"Friends?" [...]

"Yes," Rosa[...]

He did not re[...] her [...], [...] very [...], g[...]
into her upturned face, perusing her features. "With each
new day of our acquaintance," he said softly, his attention
coming to rest upon her mouth, "I become more convinced that you are the most beautiful woman I have ever
known."

Rosalind could not still the mad beating of her heart.
Every woman deserved to hear those words once in her
life, and though she did not doubt Brad's sincerity, she
warned herself not to become fanciful once again. "It is
the candlelight, sir. Females the world over know how
flattering candlelight is to us all."

"Perhaps," he said, "but you have no need of artificial
light. Your beauty is illumined by your gentle soul."

With that, he bent and kissed her hand. Softly. Gently.
Unhurriedly. The feel of his firm lips warmed her skin;
then it seemed to penetrate to her bloodstream, where it
traveled upward all along her arm, not stopping until it
reached some hitherto undiscovered place within her
chest.

When he finally looked up at her, his blue eyes were no
longer teasing, and Rosalind fancied they held just a hint
of regret. "You are a very special lady," he whispered.

Their gazes held, and with her hand still in his, he
straightened and urged her toward him. Unresisting, Rosalind took a step forward. As she waited, Brad lowered his
head and touched his lips to hers. It was a gentle kiss, yet
while it lasted, waves of warmth swept over her. Suddenly,
everything in her quiet, orderly world went spinning out
of control. . . .

Books by Martha Kirkland

THE GALLANT GAMBLER

THREE FOR BRIGHTON

THE NOBLE NEPHEW

THE SEDUCTIVE SPY

Published by Zebra Books

THE
SEDUCTIVE
SPY
Martha Kirkland

Zebra Books
Kensington Publishing Corp.

http://www.zebrabooks.com

ZEBRA BOOKS are published by

Kensington Publishing Corp.
850 Third Avenue
New York, NY 10022

First Printing: February, 1999
10 9 8 7 6 5 4 3 2 1

Printed in the United States of America

*To my daughter, Dawn Ellen Kirkland,
a young lady who likes a bit of adventure.*

Prologue

April, 1809
A French prisoner-of-war camp
five miles from the Spanish border

"Deuce take it, Sergeant Major, hold him down!"

In the near darkness of the threadbare tent, the burly soldier swore beneath his breath. "I'm doing me best, sir. 'Alf conscious 'e may be, but 'e's strong as an ox."

From one of the several hundred makeshift shelters that littered the muddied acres, a sleep-husky voice called out in protest. "Shut your mummers over there, else I'll come shut 'em for you. Can't you let a man have his dreams?"

The slender blond gentleman and the now-sweating Sergeant Major remained quite still, neither even daring to breathe. Finally, the gentleman whispered, "We must hurry, before we are discovered. The fewer people who know about this night's work the better."

"Sorry, sir, but 'e's right 'andy with 'is fives. And though 'is method be mere Lancashire, with no real science about it, still and all, 'e—damn the bugger!" he protested. " 'E tried to knee me in me privates!"

The gentleman gave what assistance he could by pressing his booted foot down hard on their fellow prisoner's right wrist, forcing it into the muddy ground. "Do what you must to subdue him, Sergeant Major. You know I cannot help you and hold the cup as well."

"I'm trying, sir. No sooner do I get 'is arms pinned down than 'e kicks me. Then I get 'is legs down and 'e—"

"Yes, yes. I see your difficulties, but this is the last of the laudanum, and if I fail to get it inside him, we might as well call off the entire plan. The fellow will never agree to do my bidding, and you and I both know it."

The wounded man, burning up with fever, had been drifting in and out of consciousness all evening, and now he moaned and tried to free himself once again. The Sergeant Major saw the fist coming and grabbed it in midair; then, to force the man into submission, he ruthlessly pressed his thumb into the fellow's left shoulder, just above the spot where the bullet had been dug out only two days earlier. At the sudden gasp of pain, the larger man whispered, "Sorry, guv."

To the slender gentleman he said, "A pox on that surgeon. 'E's a lily-livered coward, and that's the truth, but 'e's also a quack. If the Frenchies don't kill us, that sawbones will."

The gentleman shushed his confederate. "Get on with it. Time is running out, and we must finish before the emissary arrives to—"

"Corblimey!" The Sergeant Major yelped like a dog, for the man he held down had bitten him on the forearm. In pure reflex, the burly soldier drew back his large hand and brought it down sharply, cuffing the injured man across the face. The blow did the trick, for the prisoner fell back unconscious.

"Give it 'ere, sir."

The gentleman passed him the tin cup containing the last of their precious laudanum. "Do not spill it," he cautioned.

"Never fear, sir. I ain't giving this 'ere mad dog another chance to bite me."

He forced his filthy fingers between the prisoner's upper and lower teeth, prying his mouth open. Then he carefully poured the liquid down his throat. "There," he said, tossing the tin cup aside, "it's done. This 'ere bloke won't know what 'it 'im, leastways not till 'e's midway the Channel."

"I hope you may be right, Sergeant Major."

The slender gentleman retrieved the tin cup and went outside the tent where he stood quietly for some time, looking up at the pale pink streaks that had begun to lighten the dawn sky. "I pray Heaven," he said softly, "that I will be forgiven this night's work."

"You did what 'ad to be done," the Sergeant Major said, joining him in the still-crisp air. "Mark me words, sir, 'e'll thank you for it one day."

The gentleman shook his head. "I think not. My guess is, if we ever meet again, the fellow will want to slit my throat."

Chapter One

May, 1809
Whitstock, Oxfordshire

"Go to Hertfordshire! My dear Rosalind, this is all rather unexpected."

"I know, Aunt, but if I do not get away from Whitstock as soon as may be, I shall not be responsible for the consequences."

"What consequences are those, my dear?"

The plump matron lifted a pearl-handled lorgnette from where it rested upon her awe-inspiring bosom. Using the gold-rimmed glasses, she scrutinized the tall, dark-haired young woman who paced from one end of her drawing room to the other. "You may as well tell me, for I know something has occurred since last we spoke. Your color is high, and you are not acting in the least like your usual calm self. In fact, from the way you are abusing my best carpet, one might be forgiven for suspecting murder to be upon your mind."

Rosalind Hinton stopped her pacing long enough to smile at Lady Sizemore who, though on the wrong side of fifty, was still a handsome woman, with silver-streaked brown hair and blue eyes. "How well you know me, Aunt Eudora. Murder was exactly what I envisioned. And since I cannot commit such an act upon any of my nearest and dearest, I am persuaded I should get as far away from them as possible."

"Sit down, child, and tell me what is amiss. Is it my sister-in-law?"

"No. This time my mother is only indirectly involved. She contents herself with hourly reminders that as the oldest of her four daughters, and the only one unwed, it is my duty to give whatever aid and comfort I may to my married sisters."

Lady Sizemore uttered a very unladylike remark. "Say no more, for I am persuaded I can guess the rest. Your mother is pressuring you to return to Highbury with Caroline until after her confinement."

"Caroline wants it."

At her niece's confirmation of the problem, Lady Sizemore let the lorgnette fall from her fingers and reached toward a porcelain compote that rested on the tripod table beside her chair. With a precision borne of practice, she popped a sugar-coated almond into her mouth. "Caroline Hinton was ever a spoiled child," she said, crunching the nut while she spoke, "but then, very pretty children often are. Though I do not scruple to tell you, my dear, that I had hoped marrying a vicar would turn the primary object of the chit's thoughts away from herself."

"I hate to be the source of your disillusionment, Aunt,

but being Mrs. Samuel Waddell has not changed my sister one iota. She still believes that the Earth must stop spinning if she feels dizzy. And since she has become *enceinte,* she has been especially petulant."

Her ladyship made a *humph* sound. "The world is filled with women who are increasing, and most of them do not use the condition as an excuse to turn both their own and their parents' homes upside down."

Rosalind chose that moment to take the seat her aunt had offered, disposing herself upon the edge of the damask-covered wing chair. "Caroline is not most women, and she has decided she wants me with her."

"For what purpose? It is not as though she has ever shown a partiality for your company."

"No, never that. But it appears that a doting husband and four serving women are not enough to insure that her every whim is met. Therefore, she wishes our mother to exert pressure upon me to spend the next three months at the vicarage."

"Three months! Does she think you have nothing better to do than wait upon her?"

"That is exactly what she thinks."

Rosalind was obliged to take a deep breath before continuing. "My sister's exact words were, 'As a spinster, you have nothing of importance to do, so you might just as well make yourself useful to those of your family who have need of you.' "

"Why, the spiteful cat!"

"Now you see why murder was in my thoughts."

"Of course I do. One wonders only why you did not go to Lord Sizemore's gun room the instant you arrived to select a suitable weapon."

The young lady chuckled. "Aunt, I knew I could count upon you to understand me."

Her ladyship bestowed a pleased smile upon the girl who could not have been dearer to her if she had been her own daughter. "I do understand you, my dear. And I am pleased to see that you have decided to assert yourself at last. Though I say it of my own brother's family, they have never appreciated you."

"And for that," Rosalind said, "I must share some of the blame. As you have told me more than once, if a person wishes to be treated with respect, she must first respect herself. I realize now that I have been too complaisant, too agreeable."

"It comes from being a shy child. It makes one a bit guarded, reticent to venture beyond those people and places where one is comfortable."

Rosalind slapped her hand against the arm of the chair. "Well, ma'am, I am no longer a child, shy or otherwise, and from this day forth I mean to be less guarded. I know my own worth, and I am resolved to be more daring, take more risks. A mouse no more, I shall embrace adventure."

Lady Sizemore sought the lace-edged handkerchief in her reticule and waved it in salute. "Brava, my dear."

Though her cheeks grew warm at her aunt's praise, Rosalind continued. "Thanks to Caroline's careless disregard for my feelings, I saw myself through her eyes, and I realized just what my future would hold if I did not take immediate steps to change my life. If I give in this time, the remainder of my days will be spent at the beck and call of my married sisters."

"As an unpaid servant," Lady Sizemore offered, adding fuel to her niece's fire.

"Exactly! But as my family will soon discover, this is one spinster who does not mean to spend her life shuttled back and forth between households, with no home, no interests of her own. This ape leader means to find something to do with herself, starting today."

"My dear niece, I cannot tell you how pleased I am to hear it. Though, I must say," she added, "I am a bit perplexed at your wish to go to Hertfordshire. I know you dislike London, but could you not proclaim your independence at Tunbridge Wells or some other watering place where we might meet with interesting company?"

"If that is your wish, ma'am, one of the spa towns can be our ultimate destination, but only after we stop at Hertfordshire."

"My dear, what is there in Hertfordshire?"

Rosalind did not look at her aunt, but gave an inordinate amount of attention to a loose string in the thumb of her right glove. "There are the Roman ruins," she offered. "The county is famous for them."

"Rubbishy fare, my dear, and the kind of thing, I need not tell you, that bores me quite beyond the limits of my endurance. Furthermore, I take leave to doubt that the idea of visiting Roman ruins interests you one whit more than it does me. Now give over, there's a good girl, and tell me why this place has caught your fancy."

As if prepared for the question, Rosalind loosened the strings of her reticule and removed from its velvet depths a single page from a newspaper. After unfolding the printed sheet, she handed it to her aunt. "Read that," she said. "It is from *The Times.*"

Her ladyship sought the lorgnette once again and gave her attention to the topmost article. "Jubilee to begin on October twenty-fourth," she read aloud, "with a Royal fete at Frogmore. The occasion will begin the

round of celebrations in honor of the fiftieth year of
the reign of King George the third. Sources—"

"No, no," Rosalind said. "Not that article, the one
below."

With a somewhat exasperated sigh, her ladyship lowered her gaze. "Upwards of twenty thousand French
prisoners of war are now being held in England, and it
is estimated that at least ten thousand British soldiers
have been imprisoned by the French."

Because her niece remained silent, Lady Sizemore
continued, though she mumbled the words of the next
few paragraphs. "Among the two hundred men repatriated by special envoy," she said, her voice raised in
sudden interest, "is Lieutenant George Ashford, great-
nephew of Sir Miles Vernon, of Upper Stanton, Hertfordshire."

She paused, glancing at her niece, but Rosalind
merely recommended that she continue. "Lieutenant
Ashford, a member of the valiant Fifty-second Regiment
of Foot, was captured by the French during the retreat
following the battle of Corunna. Having sustained a
serious wound to the shoulder, the lieutenant has been
taken to Vernon House, the family seat in Hertfordshire,
to recuperate."

Her aunt looked up from the page, speculation lighting her eyes. "Ashford. I do not recall your ever having
mentioned such a gentleman before. Who is he? Where
did you meet him, and how long have you been
acquainted with—"

"I met the gentleman eleven years ago when I
attended the wedding of my mother's cousin, Henrietta
Willoughby."

"Eleven years! But you would have been only—"

"Fourteen," Rosalind said. "I had just celebrated my

birthday. As for Mr. George Ashford, he was already seventeen years old and bound for university the following week. He was tall, slender, and very blond, and he quoted to me from the sonnets. I thought him the handsomest young man I had ever seen.''

Lady Sizemore, being of a romantic turn of mind, placed her hand over her heart and sighed. "Eleven years, and you never forgot him.''

"I pray you, Aunt, do not rush to any conclusions. I have not laid eyes upon George Ashford since that week, and for all I know, he may not have the least recollection of me.''

"Never say so, my dear Rosalind. He will not have forgotten. I am convinced of it.''

While the ladies made plans for their trip to Hertford-shire, the owner of Vernon House instructed the footman whose job it was to push the old gentleman's wheeled chair, to move him closer to his great-nephew's bed. "I wish to have a better look at the lad," Sir Miles said.

"Yes, sir.''

When he was as close as he could get to the large mahogany four-poster, he raised a blue-veined hand to his forehead to shield his eyes from the bright light of the lamp on the bed table. Then he studied the blond-haired gentleman who lay unmoving, his face pale against the starched, white sheets. After a time, he turned his attention from the patient to the middle-aged physician who stood on the other side of the bed. "How is he, Thistlewaite?"

The soberly clad doctor made a slight adjustment to the fresh bandage he had just wound around the patient's shoulder. "I fancy the fever has abated somewhat, Sir Miles. Unfortunately, though the lieutenant has regained consciousness twice, the incidents were of short duration."

"Did he speak?" he asked, his voice far from steady. "Did he ask for me?"

Thistlewaite shook his head. "He spoke very little, sir, and in fragmented sentences. He was far from lucid. As near as I could determine, the lieutenant fancied he was still in the prisoner-of-war camp, and he was agitated about something that happened between him and a Sergeant Major. I believe he thought the other soldier meant him harm, for he tried to kick me when I applied ointment to his wound."

"The poor lad."

Sir Miles removed a linen handkerchief from inside his dressing gown and wiped the sudden moisture from his eyes. "I had hoped he might wake and ask for me. We quarreled, don't you know, over his wish to purchase a pair of colors. The lad was adamant, and I would not relent. As a result of our disagreement, I have not seen him for five years. He came to Hertfordshire just before he left for the peninsula, but I . . . I was too stiff-rumped to grant him an interview."

The physician came around the bed and placed his hand on the old gentleman's shoulder. "Do not persist in recalling past wrongs, sir, for such memories are unproductive. It is to you the lieutenant owes his life, for I know you paid dearly to have him repatriated. From what I have heard of French prisoner-of-war camps, I doubt your nephew would have survived there much longer. Another few days and his wound would have become—"

"No," Sir Miles said, raising his hand for silence. "Do

not say it, for I cannot bear to think of what might have happened."

Later, when the physician went belowstairs to have a bite of supper, Sir Miles instructed the footman to wait outside in the corridor. Once the door was shut, and he was alone with his nephew, he reached over and laid his quivering hand upon the younger man's, grasping the overly warm fingers.

The patient lay very still. His eyes were closed and his face appeared frighteningly pale, at least what Sir Miles could see of it beneath five months' growth of beard. He was no longer a lad, but a man fully grown, appearing even older than his uncle had expected. It was obvious that time, and the hardships of war, plus the ravages of illness, had taken their toll upon his youthful countenance. Oddly, only his hair seemed familiar. Though in need of a good cut, it was as straight and blond as ever, and it fell across his forehead much as it had used to do when he was a youngster.

"George, my boy, it is your uncle. Try if you can wake up."

As if his nephew had heard him, his eyelids twitched, then they opened slowly, revealing blue eyes still clouded from the laudanum.

"George, lad," Sir Miles said, squeezing the warm fingers he still held, "you are home, my boy. You are safe at Vernon House."

The blue eyes tried to focus, though it seemed to require a great effort, and the patient licked his fever-cracked lips. "Where am I?" he said, his voice raspy with disuse.

"You are home, my boy. You need worry no more, for I shall see you are given every attention. Dr. Thistlewaite is here, and he assures me you will soon be right as a trivet.''

The patient stared, as if unconvinced by the older gentleman's reassuring words. ''Where am I?'' he asked again. ''And who are you?''

Chapter Two

"Aunt," Rosalind said, exasperation in her voice, "please have John Coachman continue on to the village. The innkeeper at the Muted Swan is expecting us, and I should feel much better if we waited until morning to call in at Vernon House. After all, we have been upon the road for six hours, and I am persuaded I must look a fright."

"Nonsense," Lady Sizemore said, turning from her contemplation of the leafy lane and the woodland beyond, with its stretch of coppiced hornbeam and birch trees. "You look a picture, my dear. Your traveling dress is only a little crushed, and that dark green spencer brings out the green in your eyes. Besides, I feel certain Sir Miles will not mind if we are a bit mussed, for a friend of his nephew's must always be welcome."

"Aunt Eudora," Rosalind warned, not the least bit taken in by that last remark, "I hope you do not mean to try your hand at playing Cupid. I told you I have not seen George Ashford in more than eleven years, and for all I know, he may have a wife and at least twenty children.''

"Hardly that many, my dear. Not unless twins run in the Vernon family. The time factor, don't you know. To produce twenty children would require—''

"Thank you, I stand corrected. Now, I pray you, cease trying to divert my attention, for I know what you expect to achieve by stopping in with all manner of baggage strapped to the roof of the chaise. You imagine that proximity is all that is needed to ignite a romance between the lieutenant and me, and for that reason you hope to force his uncle to invite us to stay at Vernon House.''

"Force! Pish and tosh, my dear. As though I would do anything so shabby-genteel. However, now that you mention it, if Sir Miles should take one look at you and realize for himself the benefit such a pretty face would have upon his nephew's recovery, I hope you will not refuse to remain for a few days. A private home must always be more comfortable than an inn. Besides,'' she added, patting Rosalind's knee, "the lieutenant will not have married. Depend upon it, he will have neither wife nor child.''

Rosalind leaned her head back against the padded squabs of her aunt's slightly antiquated chaise and closed her eyes. She wished she had never suggested this trip, for the closer they got to their destination, the more rash this entire idea seemed. And to add to her disquiet, her aunt was busy plotting schemes to throw her in the poor lieutenant's path. Of course, she might have known how it would be, for in her own way, Lady Sizemore was every bit as eager as Mrs. Hinton to see Rosalind wed—if for slightly more romantic reasons.

If she were in possession of a magic wand, Rosalind would wave it now, and when she opened her eyes again, it would be tomorrow and she and her aunt would be in Tunbridge Wells. With a second wave of her wand, she would erase from Lady Sizemore's memory all conversation concerning a stop in at Hertfordshire. How unfortunate that Rosalind possessed no such wand; otherwise, she would not now be only minutes from intruding upon the life of a gentleman who probably had no recollection of her existence.

After all, why should George Ashford remember one skinny, shy schoolgirl? As handsome as he was, with the sky blue eyes of a poet and the dark blond hair of a young Lochinvar, young ladies by the dozens must have fallen in love with him. With such an abundance of admirers, it was not reasonable to assume that he would have retained the memory of a quite unprepossessing chit with little beauty and nothing to recommend her but a crooked smile and a head full of thick, dark hair.

Actually, though her aunt was convinced that Rosalind had spent the past eleven years pining over the young man, it was not true. She had not thought of him in years. Furthermore, if she had not been goaded into flight by her sister's assumption that a spinster had nothing better to do than become a dog's body to her married siblings, the article about George Ashford's return to Hertfordshire might even now be wrapped around yesterday's garbage.

But her sister had goaded her, and because Rosalind was in possession of a small income left her by her paternal grandmother, flight was possible. It was mere chance that she had seen the article on the same day she had declared herself ready to escape the confinements of her home and family—eager for a bit of adventure, a broader sphere, and a fuller life.

Chance had put the article in her hand, and the lack of a magic wand had kept her on the road, and now it was too late to repine over the decision to stop in at Hertfordshire. With no choice but to make the best of it, Rosalind took a deep breath and squared her shoulders.

The resolve came none too soon, for her ladyship's coachman had just reined in the four horses beside a wrought iron gate bounded by two enormous limestone gate piers. Atop each pier capital stood a giant eagle, its wings spread impressively, as if to guard the property. After conversing briefly with the wizened old man who came from the well-kept gray stone gatehouse, John Coachman directed the cattle past the eagles and up the short gravel carriageway.

Ignoring her own misgivings, Rosalind gave her attention to her aunt, who was leaning out the window of the chaise to get a better look at the three-story, Tudor-style mansion up ahead.

"A handsome establishment," Lady Sizemore said. "Of a good size without being pretentious. And I like the use of the gray stone. What say you, my dear?"

"It is handsome enough, I suppose." Rosalind's unenthusiastic reply was for her aunt's benefit, for she knew the lady already envisioned Vernon House as her niece's future home.

Not discouraged by such lukewarm praise, her ladyship continued. "And what marvelous views must be had from the upper story windows. I vow the house owes much of its appeal to the splendor of the grounds."

With this, at least, Rosalind could agree wholeheartedly. The carriageway bisected a beautiful expanse of lush, slightly sloping green lawn, and on either side of the house stood what promised to be exquisite formal gardens. Both gardens were surrounded by privet hedges fully five feet high, and their entrances were guarded by more of those giant carved eagles perched atop pairs of limestone pilasters.

While Rosalind gazed at those eagles, the coachman drew the chaise up to the arched portico and the postilion jumped down from the box to open the door and help the ladies to alight. Before she allowed him to assist her, however, Rosalind tried one final time to moderate her aunt's romantic enthusiasm. "To spare my blushes, Aunt Eudora, pray allow me to inform Sir Miles that we have broken our journey only for a few minutes in order to congratulate Lieutenant Ashford upon his safe return."

"If that is your wish, my dear. Though I assure you the old gentleman will find nothing remarkable in your wanting to pay your respects to a childhood friend."

"Not if he does not ask too many questions regarding the duration of that friendship."

"I am persuaded that such questions will not even occur to him. And if we are extended the hospitality of the house, we will accept. Will we not?"

Rosalind did not answer the question, but said, "Sir Miles may well be from home, and if that proves to be the situation, I will entrust to the butler the note I have written the lieutenant wishing him a speedy recovery. After that, you and I will continue to the village, and on the morrow we will resume our journey to Tunbridge Wells."

* * *

As it turned out, everyone in the house was flatteringly pleased to welcome any friend of the lieutenant's, beginning with the white-haired butler who first greeted them and ascertained their reason for calling.

"I assure, your ladyship," he said, bowing and opening the entrance door wide, "that Sir Miles will be most eager to make your acquaintance, and that of the young lady as well. If you will be so good as to step inside."

Once inside the circular vestibule, with its beige and ocher marble floor and its plaster walls painted a muted terra-cotta, they followed the servant to a small but well-appointed receiving room decorated in shades of yellow. "I shall be but a minute," he assured them. "Please make yourselves comfortable while I inform Sir Miles of your arrival."

Within minutes, Rosalind heard the squeak of wheels. She thought the noise might be that of a tea cart in need of a spot of lubricant, but when the butler reentered the room, he was followed by a tall, well-built young footman who pushed a high-backed oak chair fitted with wheels. Seated in the chair was a smallish gentleman of perhaps seventy-five years. His hair was completely white, and his skin appeared paper thin. Though he looked at them through myopic gray eyes, as though not seeing them too clearly, his smile was warm and welcoming.

"Lady Sizemore. Miss Hinton. Welcome to Vernon House."

"Sir Miles," Rosalind said, curtsying to the gentleman, "it is kind of you to receive us."

"Not at all, my dear young lady. Any friend of Ashford's is most welcome. Furthermore, you have come at a most opportune time."

"How is that, sir? May we hope that the lieutenant's health is improved?"

"You may, indeed, Miss Hinton. I cannot tell you how happy I am, for the physician has only just informed me that my nephew is completely conscious, and that his fever appears to have abated."

"That is good news," Lady Sizemore said.

"Indeed," Rosalind agreed. Controlling all but the tiniest hint of warmth in her cheeks, she recited the story she and her aunt had agreed upon. "As I told the butler, we are but passing through Hertfordshire on our way to Tunbridge Wells, and I just happened to see the article in *The Times*. We had no idea the lieutenant was in such poor health, or we would not have intruded upon your privacy."

"I assure you, young lady, it is no intrusion. And if I know young men, seeing such a pretty face as yours will be more beneficial to Ashford's recovery than all the nostrums and tonics in Dr. Thistlewaite's black bag."

Lady Sizemore gave Rosalind a telling look. "That is exactly what I was saying, Sir Miles."

"Unfortunately," the old gentleman continued, "the doctor wishes my nephew to get as much natural sleep as possible, so he has declared that no one is to enter the bedchamber but himself until tomorrow. However," he added, "if it will not interfere with your plans, perhaps you ladies would consider remaining at Vernon House for a few days. I should dislike to be the one to inform Ashford that a beautiful young woman called upon him but was unable to stay."

Rosalind was obliged to glance away, for she could not look Sir Miles in the face. She felt as if they had manipulated this kind old gentleman into the invitation.

"We should be delighted," Lady Sizemore said, "to accept your hospitality."

After their host sent the butler to see that rooms were prepared for the guests, Sir Miles told them a little of how he was able to secure a place for his nephew among the two hundred repatriated prisoners of war. "Of course, I had no notion the lad was wounded. If I had, I would have sent a nurse along to see to his care."

"Of course you would have." Lady Sizemore said all that was proper, concluding with, "Poor Lieutenant Ashford."

"My nephew was suffering from a fever brought on by the bullet wound in his shoulder, and since the emissary who escorted the repatriated men back to England was unqualified to give medical treatment, he chose to keep the lad sedated the entire trip home."

"The poor young man," her ladyship said. "How befuddled he must have felt when he first awoke. One can only imagine how the combination of fever and prolonged dosing played havoc with his senses."

"And his memory," Sir Miles added. "Why, when Ashford first opened his eyes, he did not even recognize me."

Her ladyship *oohed* in sympathy.

In this, at least, Rosalind shared her aunt's feelings. "I can think of nothing so frightening," she said, "as waking from a prolonged illness and discovering that one is unable to recall the simplest details of one's life."

Unaware that he was the subject of discussion and commiseration belowstairs, the patient was busy remembering not only his entire life, but also every detail of the mission that had been his purpose in going to the peninsula. He lay in Lieutenant George Ashford's four-poster bed, with its green velvet hangings and its green and mulberry counterpane, recalling every piece of pertinent information, and mentally listing each name, along with the date and place he had met the various junta leaders.

His eyes were fixed upon the *fleur de lis* pattern of the wallpaper, for he was employing one of the many little tricks he used to aid him in recalling long, dull lists; he was bestowing upon each of the gold-edged flowers the name of one of the guerilla leaders in Portugal and Spain. "Joao Duarte," he said aloud, "from north of Oporto. Miguel, from Aveiro. Pilar, from Torres Vedras. Thomas, from Olivenza."

Since the wall boasted hundreds of *fleur de lis,* he restricted his naming to the section just above the rosewood writing desk. When he came to the end of his list, he closed his eyes and sighed, happy to know that the long period of laudanum-induced oblivion had not robbed him of the all-important information. It was the gentleman's uncanny memory, among other talents, that had prompted the Duke of York to send Brad upon the mission in the first place, and he was thankful that his illness had not erased from his brain the pertinent names and locations.

Reassured that his months of travel through Portugal and Spain, plus his subsequent imprisonment by the French, had not been for naught, Bradford Charles Stone, the sixth baron Stone, turned his thoughts to solving the problem of getting to London to impart his hard-won information to the Duke. At the moment, of course, Brad was still weak as a kitten, but it was imperative that he get to the Duke at the earliest opportunity. Who could say how much of their future success against

Napoleon's army might rest with knowing the names and locations of the British sympathizers on the peninsula?

Since there was nothing he could do at the moment, Brad gave in to the almost overwhelming desire to sleep, and within moments of closing his eyes, he was once again folded in the warmth of healing slumber.

After a deliciously prepared dinner, during which their host ate little but conversed with Rosalind and her aunt with all the pleasure of one entertaining old friends, the ladies retired to their respective bedchambers, happy to turn in early after several hours of travel. To Rosalind's delight, when she entered the pretty blue room assigned to her, a young maid waited to assist her from her dinner dress into her chaste white night rail.

Even though the girl was so kind as to brush out Rosalind's long, thick hair and rub her temples with rose water, once she climbed into the snug, half-tester bed, sleep eluded her. For what seemed like hours, Rosalind lay in the darkness wide awake, wondering what would happen when she finally came face-to-face with the patient who slept in the bedchamber just across the corridor from her own.

The answer to that question came sooner than she had expected, for some time after midnight she heard what sounded like an argument. She might have ignored the heated discussion, had it not been for the rather curious fact that it was one-sided, with only one person participating. Stranger still, that deep voice conversed solely in French!

Curious to know what was happening, Rosalind got out of bed, shoved her arms into her white lawn wrapper without bothering to tie the yellow ribbons that secured it, and opened her bedchamber door the merest crack.

To her surprise, the door across from hers stood ajar, and a faint light showed on the carpet in the corridor. Since the room was Lieutenant Ashford's, Rosalind did not return to her bed immediately, but stood listening, wondering why no one was trying to quiet the patient.

"Merde!" the deep voice all but shouted. *"Nom de Dieu. Vous êtes un imbécile!"*

Even though Rosalind's command of the French language was faulty at best, her understanding of those quickly spoken remarks was sufficient to tell her the patient was under the influence of a powerful emotion.

"Zut alors! Cochon."

After calling someone a pig, he fell silent for a few moments.

"Sacre bleu! Je connais rien des partisans."

Partisans? How odd. Why would a soldier need to deny knowledge of such persons?

There was another silence, after which he moaned then spit out rather bitterly, *"Me lâchez, porceau."*

The patient's imaginary tormentor, who obviously did not obey the order to release him, had graduated from being a pig to being a swine.

Following that last outburst, nothing more was said for a time. When the patient spoke again, the words were in English. "I tell you, I will not do it. I wish you no harm, Sergeant Major, but—*ohhh!*"

That last was a cry of pain, whether actual or merely remembered, Rosalind was unable to discern, but she could not stand by and do nothing. Thinking only to offer what assistance she might, she hurried across the corridor toward the faint light.

"Hello," she said, knocking softly at the door.

Receiving no answer, she peered inside the dimly lit room. It was empty save for the patient. Assuming the doctor had gone belowstairs to fetch something, Rosalind approached the bed. As it turned out, her assistance was not needed, for the tall, broad-shouldered man who lay beneath the mussed green and mulberry counterpane had grown quiet. She thought he slept; however, when she reached out to pull the covers back up over his naked shoulders, she discovered her error.

Quicker than she had thought possible, his hand reached out and captured her wrist in a painful grasp, his long fingers digging into her flesh.

Startled, she stared at the thick, male forearm whose raised veins showed dark blue against his tan skin. Then she lifted her gaze to the man's unshaven face. His eyes were open wide, as if he was as surprised as she by this unexpected encounter.

"If this is a dream," he said, still holding her fast, "it is a decided improvement over the ones I have been experiencing. Those were nightmares filled with ogres sporting horns and bearing pitchforks—ogres I wish never to see again."

"Ogres," Rosalind repeated, trying for a calm voice. "And pigs, as well, I think." While she spoke, she attempted, albeit gently, to pry his thumb loose.

He lifted one dark blond eyebrow as if amused by her attempt to free herself. "Ogres. Pigs. It makes no difference, as both are forgotten now, replaced by a vision whose presence any man must welcome in his dreams, or in his arms."

His fingers tightened on her wrist, and without warning he pulled her several inches closer. Though she managed to keep her balance so that she did not fall upon his chest, her hair swung forward, brushing against his cheek. As if that had been his purpose all along, he turned his face into the thick tresses, breathing deeply. "Umm," he murmured, "you smell delicious. All warm and womanly."

The words were soft, almost seductive, and while he spoke, his gaze traveled slowly from the curve of her jaw, down her neck, and lower, to the skin revealed by her open wrapper. "Such an enticing vision," he whispered. "From the smooth, ivory skin of your throat, down to the creamy swell of your—"

"Sir!" she gasped, pulling away from him.

To Rosalind's surprise, he let her go completely, and as she jumped back, putting several feet between them, she clutched at her wrapper, holding it together. With decidedly unsteady fingers, she tied the yellow ribbons, all the while searching her brain for an explanation in case he should ask her why she was in his room in such a state of *dishabille*. Unfortunately, it was difficult to think with him staring at her in that half-teasing, half-mocking manner. His eyebrow lifted speculatively, as if he were imagining how she looked without the benefit of the chaste white night rail.

She would not give him the satisfaction of lowering her gaze, but as she traded stare for stare, Rosalind wondered how this unnerving man could possibly be the sonnet-quoting boy she remembered. Without having given her expectations much thought, she supposed she must have envisioned a man only slightly altered from the handsome, willowy youth of her recollections, albeit an invalid, reed-thin from his months of imprisonment. Nothing could have been farther from the truth.

The man before her was not at all like the person she expected. True, there was not an ounce of spare flesh upon him, but beneath his broad, powerful shoulders and rock-hard form dwelt sinewy muscles. He was more sturdy oak than slender willow.

Eleven years had changed George Ashford almost past recognition. Still in evidence was the dark blond hair she remembered, as well as the sky blue eyes, but there the similarity ended. When, Rosalind wondered, had the poetic innocence in those eyes been replaced by that smiling awareness? From whence came this disturbing male who exuded animal magnetism—exuded it and took intense satisfaction in the act?

As if he read her thoughts, his lips turned up at the corners. "Since you are a flesh and blood vision, and not one created by my fevered brain, pray tell me, my lovely, to what do I owe this visit?"

"I heard you cry out. Your door was open and the doctor was not in evidence, so I came to see if I could help. I did not mean to intrude."

"A beautiful woman is never an intrusion, my sweet. Especially in a man's bedchamber."

Rosalind felt the heat of embarrassment scorch her face. How dare he put her to the blush, when her only motive for coming to his room had been one of compassion for a fellow being. Thinking only to turn the conversation, she said, "You do not remember me, do you, Lieutenant?"

For a split second his eyes appeared wary; then, as if to cover the gaffe, he smiled, revealing strong, even teeth. "How could any man forget a lady as beautiful as you? Those sultry green eyes. Those soft, kissable lips. That ivory skin so satiny looking it tempts a man to—"

"Sir!"

It was apparent what he was doing; he was attempting to distract her with his warm compliments. And he was succeeding. Though why he should wish to discomfit her, Rosalind could not imagine. Whatever his reasons, she wished she had never come into his room, never given him ammunition with which to attack her. She was on the verge of turning and walking out when some imp prompted her to do whatever it took to wipe that smug look from his face.

"You have forgotten me," she said, her voice filled with pathos. Not finished yet, she breathed a ragged sigh, as though trying valiantly to control her emotions; then she blinked her eyelids several times as if holding back the tears. "Shame on you, George Ashford, for you have broken my heart. How could a man forget the girl to whom he had proposed marriage?"

Chapter Three

Proposed marriage? Damnation! Was Ashford engaged? The complications seemed to be mounting—first an elderly uncle who sought forgiveness, and now a heart-broken fiancée.

Brad tried to think. Had the lieutenant ever spoken of a particular young lady? No, he was positive he had not. At no time during the six months they had been imprisoned by the French had Ashford ever mentioned the existence of a fiancée, and because they had discussed anything and everything to keep boredom at bay, Brad felt sure the subject would have come up.

"Well, now," he said, stalling for time, "I agree that forgetting such a circumstance as you mention would be a shameful occurrence; however—"

"Not a circumstance," she said, a betraying light in those tantalizing green eyes, eyes he noticed showed not even a trace of the tears she had supposedly blinked back, "an engagement."

"An engagement," he repeated, deciding to brave it out. "Perhaps you could refresh my memory just a bit. Our attachment, is it of long standing?"

"Oh, yes. Quite long."

The betraying twitch of her lips did not escape Brad's notice. So, the beauty was extracting a bit of revenge for his earlier behavior. Breathing a sigh of relief, he said, "The measurement of time is such a subjective thing. What one person calls long, another may deem no more than the blink of an eye. Could you be more specific?"

"Of course," she said. "You made me the offer of your hand eleven years ago."

"Eleven years! Madam, you could not have been much more than eleven yourself."

She blushed rather prettily. "I was fourteen at the time, sir. But I . . . er . . . I was quite old enough to know my heart."

The minx. Brad did not know whether to laugh at the preposterous tale or throw his pillow at the saucy fibster. Too bad he had let her put so much distance between them, for if he had hold of her wrist now, he would know how to make her pay for such teasing.

The idea of exacting retribution upon those kissable lips, after so many months without the comfort of female companionship, made Brad's heart rate rise noticeably. Not certain that excitement was good for a man just recovering from a fever, and hoping to give his thoughts a different turn, he said, "Let me see if I understand this situation correctly, madam. You mean to bamboozle me into believing that you have lived the intervening years in expectation of one day becoming Mrs. George Ashford."

"That is correct. And though I say it myself, I believe I have shown admirable patience."

"Admirable? Madam, I should rather say your patience is remarkable."

She tried batting her eyes again, as though blinking away the tears, but the ruse was even less convincing the second time. "The sad truth," she said, "is that I have wasted my youth waiting for you to honor your commitment to me, and now I stand before you a spinster quite at my last prayers."

"I can see that, madam. At the advanced age of five and twenty, one marvels that you have not crumbled entirely to dust."

A gurgle of laughter escaped her, but it was quickly disguised by a spurious fit of coughing. Not, however, before Brad was privy to the sight of a pair of dimples. A dangerous combination that—a beautiful woman with a sense of humor. Against such formidable weaponry, a man would do well to be on his guard. Giving up all pretense, he said, "Who are you?"

"What?" she said, feigning shock. "Have you proposed to so many young ladies that you cannot even recall all their names?"

What Brad would have replied to that sally was anyone's guess, for the doctor chose that moment to enter the bedchamber. In his hands he carried a small silver tray, and upon that tray reposed an earthen mug from which emanated steam and a decidedly noxious aroma. "What is this?" he said upon spying the young lady. "The patient was to have no visitors until tomorrow. I thought I made that perfectly clear."

"I beg your pardon, doctor, and I apologize in advance if my visit should prove an impediment to the patient's recovery. Let us hope," she said, looking pointedly at the vile-smelling potion in the mug, "that you have brought just the thing to revive his lagging spirits."

Without another word, she turned and disappeared into the darkness of the corridor, leaving Brad to wonder who she was and how she had come to be involved in the life of Lieutenant George Ashford. She was not the gentleman's fiancée, of that Brad was convinced. In fact, there were no rings of any kind on her fingers. For the life of him, Brad could not imagine how a woman of such striking beauty and vivacity had managed to survive twenty-five years without being *someone's* fiancée.

The noxious liquid must have done the trick, for the next day when Rosalind met Dr. Thistlewaite in the pretty dove gray morning room with its pearl and rose Brussels carpet, the man was filled with excitement. He was happy to have an interested ear into which to relate the miraculous nature of the lieutenant's recovery. "I must see to the bottling of my recipe," he said, "for the tisane worked even better than I had hoped. Who can say but what I have found the source of my future prosperity."

"Who, indeed," Rosalind said politely.

Perceiving that the physician needed little encouragement to continue his story, she moved to the mahogany buffet where a dozen covered dishes awaited her pleasure. Taking one of the china plates stacked at the end of the buffet, she served herself a braised egg and a small piece of salmon. While she debated the choice of currant bun or a Sally Lunn, Thistlewaite continued his story.

"Though the patient refused at first to drink the

reviving potion, once I persuaded him that it was in his best interest to allow me to do my job, he swallowed every last drop." After a self-satisfied smile, the doctor added, "As a result, I am happy to report that the lieutenant slept the sleep of an innocent babe. And when he awoke this morning, he declared that he felt like a new man."

"That is good news, sir."

As Rosalind approached the table, the physician hurried to hold her chair, then he poured her a cup of coffee from the silver service and returned to his own place, all without interrupting a single word of his story. "You can imagine Sir Miles's elation, Miss Hinton, when I told him of his nephew's progress. Why, nothing would do but that he be taken immediately to the younger man's bedchamber." Thistlewaite sighed with pleasure at the memory.

"I can only pray," he added, a note of reproach in his voice, "that the patient does not suffer a relapse as a result of last night's visit."

Rosalind had just taken a bite of the Sally Lunn, but she swallowed quickly. "Is that likely, sir? Is Ashford still in danger?"

"Not if he follows my instructions to the letter. Unfortunately, he has already chosen to disregard my best advice."

"What has he done?"

"The lieutenant has called for a hip bath," he replied, the words spoken with a shudder, "and he wishes to be soaped from head to foot!"

Dr. Thistlewaite required a sustaining bite of escalloped kidneys, with an accompanying sampling of braised eggs before he could say more. "As I informed Sir Miles, I cannot be held responsible for any adverse effects resulting from the patient's insistence upon being submerged in water, especially when he has only just recovered from a debilitating fever."

Rosalind observed that the doctor awaited some sort of response from her, and choosing not to bandy words with him, she uttered a noncommittal, "Ah, yes."

Recalling that the patient in question had just spent six months in a prisoner-of-war camp, Rosalind was of the opinion that a long hot soak was precisely the medicine he needed. Keeping that medical heresy to herself, however, she asked if the submersion had, in fact, done the lieutenant any harm.

"None so far," Thistlewaite replied reluctantly. "When I came down to break my fast, Sir Miles's valet had just entered the room with a tray bearing shaving soap, a razor, and a pair of barbering scissors. I cautioned the patient, who was sitting in a chair by the window, advising him to return to his bed to ward off the effects of the bath, but I doubt my advice was heeded."

Thistlewaite tossed his napkin upon the table, the gesture dramatic enough to bring to mind the image of Pontius Pilate washing his hands of responsibility. "One can only imagine what repercussions may arise once the gentleman is shorn of his beard."

As it happened, one *was* imagining those repercussions, and that one was Brad Stone.

Brad had been eager to rid himself of all traces of the prison camp, and once the deed was accomplished, he took sybaritic delight in being clean from head to toe. Unfortunately, not until the bespectacled valet stepped back to observe his handiwork did it occur to Brad that as a result of his having been shaved and shorn, the better part of his disguise had been removed. He held his breath, waiting for the servant to sound an immediate alarm, announcing that the man before him was not George Ashford.

To Brad's surprise, nothing could have been farther from the truth. The valet, never questioning the identity of the man whose face he had bared, smiled in the indulgent manner of those servants who have known a young gentleman since his days in short coats. "That should do you, Master George," he said, removing the towel he had draped across Brad's shoulders. "I know you younger gentlemen prefer one of the modern haircuts, but I doubt your own barber could have done better."

Breathing a sigh of relief at his continued acceptance, Brad ran his fingers through his freshly shorn locks. "My own barber," he said, "will probably turn green with envy once he sees how neatly I am turned out."

"Now, Master George," the old man said, smiling in spite of his attempt not to do so, "have done with your flattery, for these are not the old days when I would slip you a sugar plum or a bit of marzipan when your uncle was not attending." While he spoke, he helped Brad into a florid dressing gown borrowed from one of the footmen, the only males in the house whose height matched Brad's own six feet.

"Speaking of food," Brad said, "I am hungry enough to eat an ox, and it makes little difference to me if the beast is still in the yoke or on the plate. I ask only that you waste no time in serving it."

The valet chuckled. "Have done with your foolishness, Master George. An ox, indeed. As though we would serve such here at Vernon House. Unless I am mistaken, Cook has prepared a nice, sustaining broth of beef and barley for you. She maintains it was always your favorite. I shall see it is brought up directly."

Brad waited quietly for the meal to be served, but after every delicious morsel was consumed, along with a tankard of excellent home brew, he began to grow restless. Months of confinement, followed by days of laudanum-induced stupor, were taking their toll upon him, making him long for activity. Though he understood that he was still too weak to set out for London on his own, he longed to be in town where he could relay to the Duke of York the information he had gathered at the Duke's bidding.

Some time later, the doctor came up to assure himself that the new bandages were comfortable and to give Brad a final examination before returning to the village. "Well, Lieutenant Ashford, you seem to have suffered no ill effects from the hip bath, and I pronounce you definitely on the mend. Having said that, however, I advise you to return to your bed and remain there for another day or two before venturing belowstairs. Even then, you would be wise to give yourself at least a fortnight before pursuing any activity more vigorous than a stroll through one of the gardens."

"I assure you, Doctor, I feel quite fit."

The physician closed his black bag with an angry snap. "Why must patients always think they know more than the doctor? What you feel, sir, is better. Not fit. Be warned, you ignore my advice at your own peril, for any imprudent exertion may well result in a total relapse."

"I shall remember your words, Doctor." He extended

his hand. "Please accept my sincere appreciation for the excellent care you have given me."

"Well, well," Thistlewaite replied, taking Brad's hand, "my pleasure, I am sure. In future, Lieutenant, mind you stay out of the line of fire."

"That advice, Doctor, I shall most definitely heed."

Before he bid the medico farewell, Brad asked if he would tell one of the servants to bring him up any newspapers available in the house. "For I should like to know what has been happening in the world."

Though the doctor bid Brad not excite himself, he nodded his agreement to relay the message. Thus, when a knock sounded some twenty minutes later, Brad expected to see one of the footmen with the newspapers. To his surprise, the bearer of a small stack of *The Times* was the young woman who had occupied a goodly portion of his thoughts since their brief encounter last night.

Unlike their previous meeting, when she was attired in nothing save a white lawn night rail and a flowing wrapper that skimmed her beguiling curves in a most tantalizing way, this time the beauty wore a modest frock of pale green sprigged muslin complete with a starched fichu that concealed those charms the low-cut dress might have revealed. As well, the marvelous sable-brown hair that had been unbound last night, free to fall where it would about her shoulders, and his, was now caught in a prim knot atop her head.

Though Brad preferred her as she had been before, she was, nonetheless, a welcome visitor. At the sight of her, he rose from the wing chair where he had been looking out the window at a handsome formal garden. "Do come in," he said. "I had begun to think you were but a figment of my imagination."

"Please," she said, "do not get up."

When he continued to stand, Rosalind pushed the door open all the way, making sure it stayed open, then she entered the room. "I understand you wish to be brought up to date on current events."

"And you have been so good as to undertake the task. I am in your debt, Madame Fiancée."

Rosalind felt the heat of embarrassment steal up her neck, warming her ears. "I beg you, do not call me that!"

Though his only response was a slightly raised eyebrow, Rosalind's own conscience smote her, reminding her of her unseemly behavior the night before. "Sir, I have brought you every paper I could find, but I will not hand them over until you promise to forgive my little jest of last evening. As you must know, I am not, nor have I ever been, your fiancée. I . . . I should not have been so forward, and my only excuse is that I let my pique run away with my good sense."

Rosalind spoke calmly enough, though she was feeling anything but calm. She had hoped this meeting would erase from her memory their previous, rather unorthodox exchange. But when she had pictured herself coming upstairs to apologize, she had not counted on the patient's almost miraculous recovery of his strength, or upon the sight of him with his clean-shaven face. It was a decidedly masculine face, with a strong jawline and a firm chin, and without the camouflage of several months of scraggly beard, his well-defined lips were revealed in a manner that caused a strange, fluttery sensation in that area just beneath Rosalind's ribs.

Furthermore, that touch of devilish delight that showed in his blue eyes when he smiled at her induced a noticeable acceleration in the beat of her heart, an acceleration so unusual Rosalind felt suddenly nervous in his company.

"So," he said, the hint of devilment still lighting his eyes, "what am I to call a lady who lets her pique run away with her good sense."

"I am Rosalind Hinton," she said, "and to refresh your memory, we did, in fact, meet eleven years ago. It was at the wedding of my mother's cousin, Miss Henrietta Willoughby."

When he showed no sign of recalling the incident, she repeated the name. "Henrietta Willoughby. I believe her brother was a particular friend of yours at Eton."

"Ah, yes, Willoughby. You must forgive me, Miss Hinton, for my mind is still a bit befogged. The delayed effect of the laudanum, no doubt."

Rosalind mumbled something noncommittal, then she turned her back to the man in the chair, using as her excuse her wish to set the stack of newspapers on the corner of a rosewood writing desk. She did not want to look into his face, nor have him look into hers, for somehow she knew he had lied.

His reply had been smooth enough, and yet, something was not quite right. Had it been the tone of his voice when he spoke the name Willoughby? The practiced way he smiled? Or the fact that the light had gone out of his eyes?

She could not say what had prompted the frisson of nervousness that had traveled up her spine, making her feel wary, and on edge, but something niggled at her brain. It was a preposterous idea, of course, and because it was so totally absurd she needed a moment to gather her wits.

Having had little experience of laudanum and its

lingering effects, she had no way of knowing if it could so adversely affect a person's memory. Somehow, though, she doubted it. It was believable enough that a man would forget an unprepossessing chit he had met once eleven years ago; however, Rosalind could not credit that a few doses of laudanum would be sufficient to cause that same man to forget the existence of a lad who had figured as his best friend for seventeen years.

She had not forgotten the knobby-kneed youth who had been so thin his acquaintances referred to him as *Stick* Willoughby. How could George Ashford have done so?

With only one objective in mind, to rid herself of the doubts that had begun to toy with her thoughts, Rosalind forced a smile to her lips and turned to look directly at the man in the wing chair. "If memory serves me, sir, I believe your young friend was addicted to sweets, and as a result was quite pudgy."

She managed to produce a credible chuckle. "You were so unkind as to dub him *Pig* Willoughby."

"Ah, yes," he said. "Now I remember. Good old Pig. When next I see my uncle, I must remember to ask him for news of my old chum."

Rosalind had made some excuse to leave the man's bedchamber. Now she sat across the corridor in her own room, with the door shut and locked, and a chair propped against it for added security. *Who was the man she had just left?* Of one thing only was she certain: he was not George Ashford.

She should have guessed it last night when she first saw him, for he was not at all like what she had expected. And it was not just that his physique was so muscular when she had pictured George Ashford as one of those persons who live and die slender; Ashford might possibly have filled out once he became an adult. No, it was something in the stranger's eyes. Something in his manner.

There was about the man an air of assurance, an unshakable confidence in his own ability; a quality Ashford never possessed. The stranger was the kind of man other men admired and were eager to emulate, and from that sultry, practiced way he had looked at her last night, Rosalind suspected he possessed those qualities that made females respond to him as well, eager to be seduced by his charm and good looks.

Why, even she had felt that flutter just looking at his chiseled lips. And with no more effort than a smile, he had caused Rosalind's heart to race, making her feel unaccountably nervous in his presence. No, the man across the corridor was nothing like the boy she had known eleven years ago.

Another thought occurred to Rosalind, prompting her to lick her suddenly dry lips. If the man was not George Ashford, then who was he? And where was Sir Miles's nephew? Had the stranger done Lieutenant Ashford an injury in order to become one of the repatriated soldiers?

At this last question, Rosalind gasped, fear gripping her, for she was struck with a terrifying thought. What if he was not, in fact, a soldier? At least, not one loyal to the British army. Was he . . . could he possibly owe allegiance to some foreign power?

She recalled the one-sided argument she had overheard last night—the troubled dream that had sent her to the man's bedchamber to see if he needed help. The argument had been spoken in French. Fluent, unaccented French.

"Heaven help us," she muttered, the words practically choking her. "The man pretending to be George Ashford must be a French spy!"

Chapter Four

Spy. Spy. Spy.

The word echoed inside Rosalind's brain, the noise building to such a crescendo she thought her head would burst from the pressure of it. If the man was a spy, then she was honor bound to expose him. As a loyal Englishwoman, she could do nothing else. And yet, what if she were wrong? So far, all was conjecture on her part. What she needed was proof of the man's duplicity. But how was she to get it?

The question filled her thoughts to the exclusion of all else, and that afternoon, when Sir Miles asked Lady Sizemore and Rosalind to join him for tea in the elegant blue drawing room, not even the handsome scagliola panels or the exquisite marble slab sofa table could claim her attention. It was all she could do to uphold her end of the conversation. That their host spoke of nothing else but his joy at his nephew's improvement only intensified Rosalind's anxiety.

As soon as the elderly gentleman excused himself, promising to meet his guests later in the dining room, Rosalind asked her aunt if she would like to take a stroll in one of the gardens.

"Thank you, no, my dear, for when I visited Sir Miles's library earlier, I discovered a novel by Maria Edgeworth that had not previously come in my way. Unless you are in need of company, I should very much like to return to my room where a quite-deliciously devious count awaits."

Devious? At her aunt's choice of words, Rosalind wished she might share her misgivings about the man abovestairs. Until she had proof, however, she was obliged to keep her suspicions to herself. Managing a smile for the lady's benefit, she said, "If a devious count is your wish, Aunt Eudora, I shall leave you to him. As for me, I am in need of some exercise and a breath of fresh air."

To Rosalind's dismay, she soon discovered that she was not the only person eager for a bit of fresh air.

Upon exiting the front entrance of Vernon House, she stepped from beneath the arched portico and paused for a moment to admire the beautiful sloping green lawn, before turning to her right and following a short flagstone path to the entrance to the east garden. The thick privet hedges that surrounded the garden were as tall as Rosalind, so when she passed through the limestone pilasters with the giant carved eagles perched atop the capitals, she felt as if she had entered a large, outdoor room.

Three major walks were laid out within the privet border. One gravel walk circled the edge of the garden, while the other two, fashioned of colored earth, ran north to south and east to west, crossing at the middle where a four-tier birdbath fully twelve feet high reached toward the sky.

Rosalind breathed deeply, enjoying the several fragrances that wafted upon the air, some divinely sweet, others delicately clean and fruity. She was looking over the entire area, trying to decide which to view first, the martagon lilies to her right or the gillyflowers and primroses to her left, when she heard the crunch of footfalls upon the gravel of the circular walk.

Turning quickly, she spied a tall man approaching from the bottom of the garden. He walked with the easy, unaffected grace of an athlete, and with the afternoon sun revealing strands of light gold in his dark blond hair, he put her in mind of one of those mythical Norse gods. He was not a god, of course, but a wolf in sheep's clothing, the spurious lieutenant, looking remarkably fit for a man supposedly injured in service to his country.

He had obviously borrowed a suit of clothes from some member of the household, but even though he wore an unremarkable brown frieze coat over equally common tan breeches, the cheaply cut garments could not disguise the muscular physique of the wearer. As he drew near, Rosalind was forced to admit that whoever he might be, the gentleman was handsome enough to break hearts.

"But not mine," she muttered, "for I know you for what you are."

"I beg your pardon," he said, raising his voice so it carried across the distance between them. "If you were speaking to me, Miss Hinton, I fear I was not close enough to hear."

Rosalind breathed a sigh of relief, warning herself to have a care. If he was what she suspected, an enemy of her country, then he was a very dangerous man. "My thoughts were for myself alone," she said when he was within speaking distance, "but if I had been addressing you, sir, I would have asked if it was altogether wise for you to have quit your bed so soon after your recovery."

He inclined his head in a negligent bow. "Your concern is quite touching, Miss Hinton, but I assure you, I am quite well."

As it happened, Brad had not spoken the complete truth. He felt more fatigued than he cared to admit, and just before he had caught sight of the lady, he had been on the lookout for a bench of some kind.

Half an hour ago, when he thought everyone was at tea and his absence would not be noticed, he had walked down to the stables to bribe one of the grooms into carrying a very private message to the coaching inn in the village. Later, as he retraced his steps, he saw a slight break in the privet hedge and forced his way through, hoping to find a shortcut to the house. Even using the most direct route, however, he found that his legs were unsteady, and he was not certain he could go much farther without a rest.

"If there is a bench," he said, "perhaps we could pause for a bit. Since I have been caught, as it were, I see no reason why I should not enjoy my fate."

Even in his weakened condition, Brad had not failed to notice the way the breeze toyed with the lady's skirts, blowing the soft muslin against her long, shapely legs. At that moment he could think of nothing he would rather do than sit in a quiet garden with this beautifully built female.

To his surprise, she looked as if she might decline his invitation, and for a moment, just before she lowered her gaze, he had detected something in her eyes that might have been fear. Not that he was put off by such a look. Fear and sexual attraction—in females the two emotions often comingled. If a man was skillful, he could soothe the former while exciting the latter.

With the ease of practice, he gave her a smile that was part flirtation, part sincere friendliness. "Lovely gardens and even lovelier ladies have not come in my way these past few months, and I have sorely missed them both. Please. Can you not find it in your heart to share just a few moments of this glorious sunshine with me? I promise I shall not bite."

After only the slightest hesitation, she pointed to a small stone bench all but hidden beneath a row of yews fashioned into topiary. "There is a likely spot, sir. Shall we avail ourselves of it?"

He offered her his arm for the short distance to the bench, and as they walked, he thanked her for agreeing to remain. "For I should like to get to know you better, ma'am."

"And I should like to know more about you, sir."

Like a warning bell, the subtle rewording of that seemingly innocent phrase put Brad instantly on his guard. When he tried to search the lady's eyes, to see if they revealed any double meaning, she lowered her lids, as though too shy to give him look for look. He was not fooled by the ploy. The lovely Miss Hinton had something to conceal, and Brad's instincts told him to beware.

Brad was a man who listened to his instincts—they had kept him alive on more than one occasion. Those instincts were talking to him now, telling him that the lady had agreed to sit with him for reasons of her own— reasons that had nothing to do with a bit of flirtation to pass a sunny day in May.

He waited until she had disposed herself comfortably on the cool stone before he took his place beside her. "Now," he said, turning to look her squarely in the face, his intent to disarm her with his openness, "ask me anything you like. My life is an open book, you may turn to whichever page interests you."

When her eyebrows lifted in surprise, Brad knew he had been wise to begin his defense with an offensive move.

"A most magnanimous invitation, sir. I shall not, however, peruse those pages recording your months as a prisoner of the French, for I am persuaded that time must be filled with memories you would prefer to forget."

"True," he replied. "I should like to forget them all—all save that moment when I opened my eyes and found myself in my room at Vernon House, with an angel standing beside my bed." He leaned toward her slightly, lowering his voice almost to a whisper. "An angel in white whose vibrant brown curls spilled down her back, the strands as luxurious and shiny as the costliest sable."

As he had expected, her cheeks turned pink at the whispered compliment. Though she tried to pretend she was unaffected by his nearness, he noticed that her bosom moved up and down at a quickened pace, her breathing shallow.

"So," she continued, moving away from him just the tiniest bit, "since we are agreed not to discuss unpleasant subjects, I shall ask you to tell me of your days at university. Oxford, I believe."

Oh, no, my lovely, you'll not trip me up with that little trick.

Brad's instincts had been correct, the lady had a plan in mind. Damnation. He must have made some sort of slip earlier, and now she suspected that he was an imposter. Not that he was worried; she could ask any question she liked and she would discover nothing from him. She was not devious enough to play the game with a real master.

Fortunately, Rosalind Hinton was a sensible woman, not one of those females who spoke without thinking. She would need proof that her suspicions were founded in truth before she said anything to Sir Miles.

He ignored the question about Oxford. "From the first moment I saw you," he said softly, "I decided yours were the loveliest eyes I had ever seen."

She blinked, as though surprised by the comment, and if she had not been such a beauty, Brad might almost have believed she was unaware of her allure. "Sir," she said, her voice slightly breathless, "you said I might ask—"

"Quite lovely," he continued. "Do you know what they remind me of?"

She shook her head. "What?"

The single syllable was barely audible and uttered almost against her will, and for just a moment he felt a pang of conscience for deceiving her. Fortunately, the moment passed quickly, for he could not afford to let himself be distracted.

"Have you ever noticed the underside of a newly blossomed oak leaf?" he asked. "The leaves are yellow-green on the top, but underneath they are a warm, rich green that always puts me in mind of lush velvet. Just like your eyes."

When she said nothing, he reached up and eased the tip of his forefinger along her jaw from just below her ear to her chin. "Your skin, on the other hand, is like satin. Smooth, cool, ivory satin. And your lips are like the petals of a rose ... pink and moist and deliciously full." He leaned closer until his mouth was mere inches from hers. "Full," he repeated, "and begging to be kissed."

"Sir!"

Rosalind stood quickly and moved several feet away from him, wondering what had just happened. A man she suspected of being a French spy had been about to kiss her, and she had very nearly allowed him to do so.

How it had progressed to that point, she had no notion. One minute she was in control, asking him questions, hoping to lead him into revealing his true identity, and the next moment he was the one doing the controlling, with her hanging onto his every syllable.

Apparently she had been mesmerized by his nearness. Without a doubt she had been beguiled by his voice— by words so sweet any female could be forgiven for falling under their spell.

"Is something amiss?" he asked, standing, but remaining beside the stone bench. "Are you unwell, Miss Hinton?"

Bewitched, more like. And well you know it!

The man's voice had held just the right note of concern, but Rosalind could swear she detected a light of triumph in his eyes. With a ferocity she had not known she possessed, she longed to box his ears until that light was extinguished. Lucky for him, she was deterred from acting out this violent fantasy by the sudden appearance of one of the footmen, who approached them at a run.

"Lieutenant Ashford," he called the minute he spied them, "Sir Miles was worried for your safety. He went to your bedchamber to see how you were faring, and when he found the room empty, he set the house at sixes and sevens searching for you."

The young servant paused only long enough to catch a much needed breath. "If you please, Lieutenant, allow me to escort you back to the house before the old gentleman is completely overset."

"Of course," he said, agreeing much too readily. "Take me to my uncle without delay."

Rosalind was not fooled by the rogue's spurious concern for his supposed uncle. Unfortunately, since she could say nothing in front of the servant, she was obliged to hold her peace and return to the house as well, with no more proof of her suspicions than she had possessed an hour earlier.

The situation within the household was as chaotic as the footman had described it, with what appeared to be the entire staff congregated in the vestibule, all of them jubilant at the return of the man they believed to be George Ashford. Because everyone was interested solely in the imposter's well-being, they paid scant attention to Rosalind; therefore, she was able to slip up to her room without the necessity of answering a single question. It was only when Lady Sizemore knocked at her bedchamber door just prior to the dinner hour that the subject of Rosalind's own sojourn in the garden was introduced.

"I vow, my dear," her ladyship began, "you are in excellent looks tonight." She lifted the lorgnette from her plump bosom, surveying the younger lady's dinner dress with its understated square neckline and its short, ruched sleeves. "You should wear yellow more often. That jonquil-colored lustring is vastly becoming to your complexion."

"Thank you, Aunt."

Deciding she had been the recipient of enough compliments for one day, Rosalind said nothing more, concentrating instead upon tying the ribbons of her matching satin slippers. The task completed, she rose from the dressing table and walked to the door, holding it open so her aunt could exit before her.

"Such a pother over that business this afternoon," Lady Sizemore said.

"What business is that?" Rosalind asked, feigning disinterest. "I am sure I do not know to what you refer."

"Why, to that little walk in the garden. From all the fuss and bother, one would have supposed such a thing had never been done before."

She winked at her niece, then looked to both right and left as if to assure herself there was no one in the corridor to overhear their conversation. "While you were among the flowers, my dear, did the lieutenant steal a kiss?"

"He is not the—"

Rosalind caught herself just in time. Both annoyed and embarrassed by her aunt's question, she had spoken without thinking. Another second and she would have revealed her suspicions that the man was not Lieutenant Ashford.

"Not what?" her ladyship asked.

"Er . . . he is not one of the heroes from Mrs. Edgeworth's novel. Quite the opposite, actually."

"You mean he did not try to kiss you?"

Rosalind hesitated only a moment. "Of course not," she lied.

"Phoo! What a disappointment. If a man cannot fill the part of a hero, the least he can do is enliven a lady's day by being a bit of a rascal."

"Aunt Eudora!"

"Do not turn missish, my dear. I did not mean that he should act a cad, merely show a bit of wickedness, like that deliciously devious Count Avedon in Maria Edgeworth's book. A fascinating fellow, the count. And never dull.''

Rosalind made no reply. She had declared that the man abovestairs was no hero; she had said nothing about his being dull. Actually, she wished he had proven to be uninteresting, for since their meeting in the garden, the counterfeit lieutenant had not been far from her thoughts.

For the two hours since she returned to her bedchamber, Rosalind had thought of little else but what had passed between them. She had become convinced that the entire encounter—the sweet words, the flirtation, the near kiss—had all been part of a plan. Its purpose had been to divert her attention, to make her forget about the questions she had meant to ask the imposter.

Somehow, the man must have guessed that she wished to trick him into revealing his true identity, and he had used his skill at seduction to distract her. And heaven help her, she had been distracted. Honesty compelled her to admit that she had fallen under his spell with embarrassing ease, drinking in the pretty compliments, growing quite breathless at the mere touch of his finger along her jaw, and eagerly awaiting his kiss.

"Like some love-starved spinster," her sister Caroline would say. But then, what did Caroline know of the matter? Her sister was married to a vicar, the worthy Mr. Samuel Waddell. She had no knowledge of the kind of men whose stock and trade was seduction—men of intrigue who with a word, a look, could make a woman's knees turn to water and make her heart race until it felt as though it might escape her chest.

Rosalind knew all too well how persuasive such men

could be. It was the memory of her own susceptibility to the imposter that now fueled the fires of her indignation. Strangely, she was not nearly as angry at him for trying to beguile her as she was at herself for being so easily beguiled.

Her composure was stretched to its limits later at the dinner table, for Sir Miles could speak of nothing but the virtues of his nephew. "George is pluck to the backbone," he said, "and though I admire his spirit, I gave him a severe scold for going out of doors this afternoon.

"I am happy to say," he continued, turning first to Rosalind on his right, then to Lady Sizemore on his left, "that the lad took the dressing down with good grace. He even went so far as to climb back into bed in deference to my wishes."

Rosalind only just stopped herself from making a rude remark. If that scoundrel had acquiesced to anyone's wishes, it was because to do so served his own purpose.

Just thinking about his duplicity made it difficult for her to swallow more than a few bites of the apricot fritter upon her plate, and under no circumstances was she calm enough to partake of the cod cakes drizzled over with oyster sauce. "Sir Miles," she said, interrupting the old gentleman's continued praise of his nephew, "I believe you told my aunt and me that until this week, you had not seen Lieutenant Ashford for five years."

"That is correct, Miss Hinton."

"I wonder, sir, do you find him much changed from when you saw him last? I must admit he looks older than I had expected. Far more mature. His appearance is more like that of a man with thirty or even thirty-one years to his credit, rather than one of only twenty-eight summers. Would you not agree? And—"

"Rosalind, my dear," Lady Sizemore interrupted, "you cannot have forgotten that the young man has been imprisoned. Such experiences must age anyone beyond his years."

Their host lifted his wineglass, turning the intricately cut goblet as if to study the play of the candlelight from the chandelier upon the crystal. Blue, gold, and red sparkled as he twirled the stem between his fingers. "Like you, Miss Hinton, I was dismayed when first I looked upon his face, for as you say, he has changed.

"I, too, noticed those undeniable alterations in his appearance, and the fact that he seems older than might be expected under normal circumstances. For just a moment, I wondered if a mistake had been made, a mix-up of some sort whereby my nephew was taken to another home and a stranger brought to Vernon House."

Rosalind studied the old man's face. "But you no longer think that?"

He shook his head. "Any misgivings I may have had were laid to rest when my valet found the coins sewn in the lad's jacket."

"What coins are those? I do not understand, sir."

"It is a trick I myself taught him. In my youth, when I traveled outside the country, I always had ten gold coins sewn inside the lining of my coat in case of emergencies. One never knows when one may be set upon in some foreign land and robbed of one's purse. Gold is the universal language, don't you know, and if a man has a bit of it, he is never totally destitute."

He set the goblet down on the snowy linen without having taken so much as a sip of the wine. "At my insistence, my valet took the lad's tattered clothing away to be burned, but before he tossed the coat onto the fire, he bethought himself to check the lining. Sure enough, there were ten gold coins sewn inside. After that, I had no more doubts."

Rosalind refrained from telling the old gentleman that every highwayman worthy of the name knew to give his victims a good patting down to search for coins sewn into their clothing. It was not a particularly innovative practice.

"He is my nephew," the old gentleman repeated, almost as if needing to believe the assertion. "He is George Ashford."

"Of course he is," Lady Sizemore said. "Who else would he be?"

Who else, indeed? Since Rosalind had no wish to upset the old gentleman without solid proof of her accusations, she held her tongue for the remainder of the meal. To her relief, the new topic of discussion embraced by their host and Lady Sizemore—a discussion upon the curative powers of the waters at Bath as opposed to those of Tunbridge Wells—required of Rosalind only the occasional comment.

"How interesting," she said more than once, though she had heard very little of what was said by either of her companions.

After dinner, while the threesome took tea in the blue drawing room, Sir Miles displayed for their edification a handsome case made of tooled Moroccan leather containing a pair of antique dueling pistols. "Notice the chased gold grips," he said, lifting one of the weapons from its felt-lined bed. Such refinements were wasted upon the ladies, who knew nothing of weaponry and cared even less about the subject, but the gentleman needed only an *ooh* of admiration from his audience to continue.

"I bought the pistols six years ago for my nephew's twenty-first birthday. To my regret, I never had an opportunity to give them to him, for the occasion came and went while we were estranged."

Their host was silent for several moments, and when he spoke again, his voice was thick with emotion. "I had the pair cleaned and polished just this afternoon. Now that the lad is returned to me, I mean to see he gets his gift." Having said this, the old gentleman closed the leather case and set it on the piecrust table at his elbow.

Within a very few minutes, Sir Miles thanked the ladies for their company at dinner, then he rang for the footman to come take him to his bedchamber. The squeaky sound of his wheeled chair had only just faded into the distance when Rosalind bid her aunt a good night and hurried up to her own room. She was eager to know if the man whose room was across the corridor from her own had, indeed, obeyed his uncle and gone to bed like a dutiful nephew.

As she suspected, he had not, for a faint light showed under his door. Rosalind paused beside that door, her breath suspended, and listened for any sound. All was quiet save for a scratching not unlike that of a quill moving across paper.

The writer paused, his right hand suspended above the ink pot, the quill ready to be dipped into the black fluid. He thought he had heard a sound just outside in the corridor. Not that he need worry. If someone should enter his room without first asking permission, all he would discover was a man sitting at a desk, writing a letter. The content of the missive would remain a secret until read by Sir Miles, the person to whom the communication was directed.

Brad had seen how upset the old gentleman was this afternoon when he discovered that the person he thought was his nephew had gone outside without telling anyone his intention. He would not do that to Sir Miles a second time, for he had no wish to be responsible for further strain upon the kindly old gentleman's health. Now that he was leaving, Brad felt he owed George Ashford's uncle some sort of explanation for having taken advantage of the care and attention meant for the lieutenant—or as much of an explanation as he could give without betraying his mission.

He hoped it was enough to attest that Ashford was in good health, and that he had seen fit to allow Brad to be repatriated in his stead because of the bullet wound. No point in relating the particulars of how he had received that wound.

When he had revealed as much as he dared, Brad thanked Sir Miles for his kindness and promised him that he would do all within his power to see that Ashford was returned to Vernon House with all possible speed. The promise made, he signed himself simply, *A friend of Lieutenant George Ashford.*

After he sprinkled the single page with sand, blew it clean, then folded it and sealed it with a wafer, he placed it upon the topmost of the bed pillows where it would be found in the morning and delivered to Sir Miles. The task completed, Brad donned the borrowed breeches and frieze coat and put the remaining nine gold coins in his pocket. He then extinguished the candle on the bedside table, plunging the room into darkness.

It was early yet, with more than an hour to wait, but he went over to the window, pulled aside the heavy drapery, and stood in the embrasure, watching for the signal.

Chapter Five

One light. Two lights. At last, there was the signal. The coachman had done as instructed and now waited in the lane just outside the wrought iron gates. Knowing the time for action had come, Brad felt that familiar surge of excitement heating his blood. Only two things had this effect upon him: making love with a beautiful woman and danger.

Grabbing up the outmoded greatcoat he had found hanging in Ashford's chiffonnier, Brad exited the room and made his way down the broad staircase, testing each step for betraying squeaks before putting his weight on it. Though all the candles in the corridor had been extinguished for the night, a full moon shone through the tall windows of the yellow receiving room off the vestibule. The moon's soft glow offered sufficient illumination for a man of Brad's nefarious talents to descend the stairs without difficulty.

Unfortunately, the entrance door proved an unexpected stumbling block. It had been locked by key from the inside, and though Brad searched in the drawer of the console table, then ran his fingers over the lintel above the door, he found nothing. Deciding the butler must keep the key on his person, he muttered an oath, then looked about for another exit.

Nothing if not resourceful, he hurried to the receiving room, where he unlocked one of the windows, raised the sash, and slipped out into the cool night air. Knowing better than to make a mad dash across the moonlit lawn, he remained hid in the shadows of the portico for a full minute until he was convinced that no one else was out and about.

Moving at last, he skirted the gravel carriageway, preferring to walk upon the much quieter grass, then he strolled unhurriedly to avoid arousing suspicion if anyone should be watching. While he covered the short distance from the front entrance to the two enormous limestone gate piers, atop which perched giant eagles, their wings spread wide as if ready for flight, Brad kept his attention focused upon the gatekeeper's small gray stone house. To his relief, no light showed in any of the windows, and he was able to slip through to the lane unchallenged.

Just beyond the gates, the coachman waited, reins in hand, on the box of an ancient post-chaise that had seen better days. There were no outriders, so the driver was obliged to remain up top to keep the pair of job horses in line. "Ho, there," he called softly, leaning over the side far enough to look down at Brad. "You the gentleman as sent the stable lad with the note and the gold coin?"

"I am," Brad answered, opening the door to the

carriage and preparing to climb inside. "How quickly can we get to London?"

Rosalind knew the minute the spy left his bed-chamber. She had been waiting for the sound.

After dinner, when she had seen the light under his door and heard the scratching of the quill across the paper, she had known instinctively that he was up to something. What it was, she could not even guess, but whatever he had planned, she knew she must do all within her power to thwart him. The safety of her country might well depend upon her actions.

With that burden weighing heavily upon her, she dismissed the housemaid who had waited up to help prepare her for bed, saying she wished to read for a while and would undress herself when she felt sleepy. Once the servant was gone, Rosalind blew out the candles, drew a chair up to her door, and waited quietly, listening for any movement in the corridor.

More than an hour passed before her vigilance was rewarded. A nearly inaudible creak, like that of a hinge in need of oil, sounded in the stillness, verifying that the door across from hers had been opened and closed. Though Rosalind did not detect even one footfall, intuition told her the spurious lieutenant walked toward the stairs.

She waited until he had progressed to a point where he was beyond hearing her movements, then she eased her own door open and tiptoed out into the darkened corridor.

Had she not been sitting in the dark for so long, she might have been unable to see, for all the candles had been extinguished. By trailing her fingers along the wall for guidance, she was able to move slowly and cautiously without mishap. When she peeped around the staircase wall, she saw a pool of moonlight from the windows of the yellow receiving room. In the midst of that light stood the spy.

Because he wore a greatcoat, she was convinced that his plans included more than a midnight stroll in the garden. Furthermore, he was running his hands along the lintel above the door, as if searching for something. Whatever he sought, he did not find it, for he muttered an oath beneath his breath then hurried to the receiving room. Moments later Rosalind heard the click of a window lock, then a sash being raised.

She allowed a full minute before she crept down the stairs, moving straight to the open window. Somehow, she was not surprised to see the spy walking purposefully toward the entrance gates. It required no special measure of deductive reasoning to determine what he was about. He meant to escape!

Knowing she must stop him, and quite certain he would not be deterred from his objective unless force was brought to bear, she turned and ran to the blue drawing room, not caring now who might hear her. To her relief, the tooled leather case still lay on the piecrust table where Sir Miles had put it earlier, and the pretty dueling pistols still reposed innocently in their felt-lined beds.

It mattered little to Rosalind that the powder flask and shot pouch were missing from the case, for she had no idea how to load and prime such a weapon. As she took up one of the pistols, a perverse sort of logic convinced her that the spy would not suspect her deficiencies. Surely such a man would never believe anyone fool enough to come after him with an unloaded pistol.

Choosing not to waste time by waking one of the servants to seek assistance, Rosalind ran back to the front drawing room and climbed out the window as the spy had done. She could no longer see him, but she took a page from his book and remained on the grass. Her destination—the gatehouse. When she spied him again, he stood beside a hired carriage. His hand was on the handle of the door, and he was preparing to climb aboard. As it transpired, the coachman had other ideas.

"Not so fast, if you please, sir," the driver said. "Beggin' your pardon, I'm sure, but 'fore I drive so much as a mile toward Lunnon, I got to see the second coin I was promised in the note."

The spy, obviously annoyed by the delay, said something Rosalind did not hear, but the driver remained resolute, determined not to move so much as an inch without further pay. "There's many a gentleman wot'll promise extra gelt," he said, "especially if a fellow's willing to drive 'im to town in the dead of the night. But only let 'im reach Lunnon, and some of them toffs'll try to diddle an honest coachman out of 'is fare."

Rosalind did not blame the coachman for being suspicious. Night driving, or black work, as it was called, was not without danger. The only people who risked traveling in the darkness were fools and those with something to hide.

Without another word, the spy dug into his pocket for the promised money. "Here you go," he said, flipping a coin high into the air.

While the driver caught the coin, Rosalind slipped through the gates. She paused only a few feet from the man she had followed; then, taking a deep breath, she raised the dueling pistol, aiming it at a spot in the middle of his broad back.

Though she was certain she had not made a sound, he grew quite still, as if all his energy was concentrated upon listening, aware of impending danger. He did not move by so much as a hair, and yet, Rosalind sensed a change in him, an alertness like that of a wild animal whose survival depends upon how quickly he can be ready to spring into action.

Menaced by the aura of raw power just waiting to be unleashed, Rosalind felt her knees begin to shake. Her hands trembled as well, so much so that she feared she might drop the weapon. Hurrying before her courage failed her, she said, "So, you mean to flee, do you? I am afraid I cannot let you do that."

He turned around slowly, looking first at the pistol, where silvery moonlight glistened off the golden handle, then finally lifting his gaze to Rosalind's face. His countenance showed neither surprise nor fear. He appeared so unruffled one might be forgiven for supposing the two of them stood on a village street filled with passersby and that Rosalind had just stopped him to ask the correct hour.

"Mind what you are about," he said, his manner relaxed, "for dueling pistols are notoriously unstable. They have been known to go off with only scant pressure upon the trigger."

Rosalind had not expected such calm. It unnerved her. "That being true," she said, the words all but sticking in her throat, "you would be well advised to do as I say and remain perfectly still."

Since he had not moved by so much as a hair's breadth, she felt a fool giving him such an order. Hoping to emphasize the seriousness of her threat, she straightened her arm, pointing the pistol directly at his heart. "I am a loyal Englishwoman," she said, "and as such, I will not hesitate to shoot an enemy of my country."

At her words, the coachman leaned over the side of the box to see what was happening. "Wot's this?"

The spy ignored him. "You speak with surprising fervor, Miss Hinton. Am I to understand that you have shot men before?"

This was not going at all the way Rosalind had envisioned it. The man seemed to have no respect for the fact that she had him at gunpoint. "Actually, I have never shot anyone. Not so far," she added quickly.

"If that is the case, then I should warn you that you may find it a more difficult task than it sounds. Furthermore, living with the consequences of such a deed is not as easy as one might think."

"I—I am prepared to live with whatever happens."

He lifted a questioning eyebrow. "Are you, now? You would have me believe that the idea of being responsible for a man's death does not bother you?"

"N—not at all."

"And what of the dreams?" he asked quietly. "What of the mental pictures one retains? Be warned, for they will bother you. The memories fade during the daylight hours only to return in the silence of the night, and when they return, they rob even the most hardened person of sleep and peace of mind."

With no more light than was offered by the moon, Brad could see that she had paled at his words, and now her entire arm shook. If he was not careful, she would shoot him by accident. To guard against that very real possibility, he needed to relieve her of the pistol, and the sooner the better.

Speed was of the essence for another reason: it might

well be that someone had followed the lady, and it was equally possible that the follower might be in possession of a more substantial weapon. Suddenly uneasy, in case that unknown person had none of Rosalind Hinton's inexperience, and none of her qualms about using him for target practice, Brad decided it was time to end this present farce and be on his way.

Moving quickly, and without warning, he brought his right hand up under hers, grasping her wrist ruthlessly tight and forcing her to turn the barrel of the pistol so it pointed upward, where no one could be shot inadvertently.

" 'Ere, now," the driver said, his voice raised in alarm. "I'll take no part in such goings on as this, gold coins or no."

Disregarding both the driver and the pain that had begun to surge through his wounded shoulder, Brad used his left hand to wrest the pistol away from her. The transfer of ownership required less than three seconds, too short a time for the lady to do more than stare at him, her eyes wide with surprise.

"You should not have straightened your arm," he said. "It put you within my reach."

Still holding her by the wrist, Brad gave a quick tug that pulled her none-too-gently against his chest; then he slipped his arm around her waist, holding her fast. "And now, my sweet, before I take my leave, I mean to extract a little payment for the inconvenience you have caused by your untimely—"

He stopped short, for the lady had taken a deep breath, and if he was any judge of the matter, it was not for the purpose of sustaining the threatened kiss. She meant to employ the weapon she should have used from the onset; she was about to scream at the top of her lungs, bringing who knew how many of Sir Miles's people to her aid.

Acting quickly, Brad tossed the pistol aside and clamped his hand over her mouth. Immediately she began to fight him, kicking at his shins and using her free hand to lash out at him, apparently not caring one iota that she was pommeling his wounded shoulder.

"Gor blimey," the coachman muttered. Not unlike a rat deserting a sinking ship, he scurried back into his place on the box, where he wasted no time in fetching his whip and cracking it above the heads of the waiting job horses. The startled team reacted immediately, straining at the traces and ready to take the weight of the carriage.

Brad was all too aware that his transportation was about to leave without him, and with no time to think what was best to do, he tossed the fighting she-cat into the moving coach and jumped in after her. The horses galloped away like a pair fleeing the fires of hell, and as a consequence, the speeding vehicle had bumped halfway down the rough lane before Brad could right himself enough to yank the door shut.

"Let me out of here!" Rosalind yelled. While she lay on the floor where she had landed originally, unable to right herself, insult was added to injury when the bouncing carriage pitched the man on top of her. "Let me out, I say."

When he ignored her order, she balled her hand into a fist and gave him a sharp blow to the side of his head.

"Deuce take it!" he said, using his forearm to ward off the next blow. "Desist."

"Then get off me, you lout!"

"Madam," he said, "if nature bestowed an ounce of intelligence upon you, try using it now. As much as you may dislike your present position, I cannot think it would be improved by my treading upon some part of your anatomy."

Though she was humiliated and incensed, Rosalind was able to see the logic of his observation. "I give you ten seconds," she said, the words spoken between clinched teeth, "after that I will . . ."

"You will what?"

The tone of his voice had not changed in any noticeable way, and in the darkness it was impossible to see his face, yet Rosalind felt a sudden chill run up her spine.

"Do not try me too far," he said softly.

At his threat—she could call it nothing else—Rosalind grew still beneath him. The sudden realization of where she was, and with whom, chased away her indignation and left in its place ever-increasing anxiety. What in heaven's name had she gotten herself into?

A bit late to be asking that question, she decided. If she truly sought answers, she might consider asking the powers above to reveal to her just what sort of madness had prompted her to pursue this man. The veriest widgeon would have shown better sense!

She pressed her lips together to stifle the groan that threatened to escape her. The man was a French spy. If what she had heard of such men was true, they thought nothing of disposing of those people who were so unwise as to get in their way.

"Do not try me too far," he had said. Was that his way of telling her that he would not hesitate to kill her? She prayed it was not, but if that was his plan, there would be no one to stop him from executing it, not once they left the neighborhood.

It was of little comfort to her that she had no one

but herself to blame for her present predicament. Her own rash behavior had put her in the spy's power, for she had chased after him without giving a thought to what might be the result of such impulsiveness. She had left her aunt, and the protection of Sir Miles's household, without saying a word to anyone. It would be mid-morning before Lady Sizemore even thought to wonder where her niece might be.

While Rosalind had been bemoaning her imprudent actions, her captor had managed to push his way up onto the seat. Now she felt his hands on her arms, pulling her up and onto the seat opposite him. "Might as well sit back and be comfortable," he said.

"Before I murder you," she added mentally, for she did not doubt that was what he was thinking.

"Actually, sir, I . . . I should be more comfortable if you would instruct the driver to set me down at the next village."

"What? Abandon a lone female in the middle of the night? Your opinion of me is low, indeed, madam, if you believe me capable of such behavior."

"I do not mind, sir, truly. I am quite resourceful."

"Nonetheless," he said pleasantly, as though insisting upon carrying her packages following a shopping expedition, "I cannot do as you ask. Who can say what disagreeable incident might befall a lady in such a situation?"

If Rosalind had not been so frightened, she might have laughed. Was he making a May game of her? Did he not number being mauled about and kidnapped among his list of disagreeable incidents?

Not that she could tell what went on in the mind of such a man. He was obviously a consummate actor, for he had convinced Sir Miles that he was George Ashford.

Why, he had even caused Rosalind to experience a moment of real sympathy for him, and that while she had held him at gunpoint.

He had asked her if being responsible for a man's death would bother her. Then he had mentioned bad dreams and the kind of memories that robbed a person of sleep and peace of mind. The words had sounded sincere, as though his own recollections were of a soul-wrenching nature. Thinking he spoke of his own pain, Rosalind had felt compassion for him.

Now, of course, she wondered if there had been any sincerity in his words. Did he, in fact, suffer from memories best forgot or had he merely waxed dramatic for her benefit?

Whatever the truth of the matter, she was not to know it, for the coach had come to the main road and the horses began to slow their pace. Recalling that the driver had tried to abandon his passenger in the lane outside Vernon House, Rosalind felt renewed hope that he might be thinking of returning to the village of Upper Stanton. If that was his intention, then perhaps she could make her escape when they reached the inn yard.

As if the spy, too, had read the driver's thoughts, he let down the window and leaned out. "London is to the west," he shouted. "You know it and I know it. So if you value your life, coachman, you will turn in that direction now. Take heed, for if you so much as slow down again before we reach town, you have my word upon it, I will shoot you the moment the coach comes to a stop."

Shoot him? Was the spy in possession of a weapon? Rosalind had not thought so. Still, his threat was enough to convince the driver. After only a moment's hesitation, the fellow turned the horses westward and cracked the whip above the team's heads to speed them on their way.

London was at least twenty-five miles from Upper Stanton, and for most of the two-and-a-half hours required to cover that distance, Rosalind remained quiet. Her head tilted back against the rough squabs, her eyes shut tight against the sight of the man who sat opposite her in the dim interior. She was cold and frightened, and she longed for the comfort of a good cry. Not that she would give in to that self-defeating indulgence, of course, for if there was any hope of her surviving this ordeal, she would need her wits about her.

Escape was impossible at the moment, while the coach sped along at better than ten miles per hour, but when they arrived in London, an opportunity might present itself. If that should happen, she would need a plan, and to devise a plan, she must remain calm and concentrate upon the realities of the situation.

The element of surprise must, of course, be a part of her design. The man was quick, and he was strong—very strong. Rosalind had ample proof of that fact. Had he not tossed her into the coach as though she weighed no more than a valise?

"Sir," she said, trying for a calm tone, "I am persuaded that the wisest plan would be for me to get out at some respectable inn on the outskirts of town. Then you will not be encumbered by an uninvited companion on the remainder of your journey."

"Interesting that you should speak of wisdom, madam, for I was only this minute thinking how limited a roll that factor has played in tonight's debacle. So far this evening, neither you nor I have acted with any degree of prudence." He stared at her through the dimness, as if trying to read her thoughts. "You certainly showed little wisdom when you pursued me with a pistol. Are you always so rash?"

Rosalind was hard pressed not to groan at the irony of that question. "You may find it difficult to believe, sir, but in my entire life, this is the first time I have acted with anything but caution."

Though he said nothing, he looked as if he doubted the assertion. After a short period of silence, he spoke again. "As to your suggestion about stopping at an inn on the outskirts of town, I have given the subject some thought, Miss Hinton, and it is not a bad idea."

For a moment, Rosalind's hopes soared, only to be brought back to earth by his next words. "I believe it would be best if we procure a room for the remainder of the night."

At his suggestion, something akin to panic shot through Rosalind. She had said nothing about procuring a room, especially not one for the two of them. She tried to keep the sound of rising hysteria from creeping into her voice. "For whom would it be best?"

"Best for all concerned."

He hesitated, as though weighing his words. "I have information that must be relayed to someone, but I doubt the gentleman would appreciate being awakened in the wee hours of the morning. Therefore . . ."

Information? Gentleman? In her desire to save herself, Rosalind had forgotten that her country was in peril. The man was a French spy, and by his own admission he had an assignation with some nefarious contact.

A lump formed in Rosalind's throat, threatening to choke her. If the information he meant to relay was used to destroy the lives of unsuspecting British soldiers, she would never forgive herself. What an arrogant fool she had been. When she first began to suspect the man of being an imposter, she should have told someone—someone powerful enough to detain him. What folly to think she could capture a spy by herself.

She swallowed with difficulty. Arrogance and vanity had led her into this predicament. This is what came of letting her wounded pride provoke her into acting without thinking. Her present precarious situation was entirely due to her having fled her home and family to avoid becoming the old maid aunt her mother and sisters seemed to believe was the acceptable fate of an unmarried woman.

"Therefore," he continued, bringing her thoughts back to the conversation at hand, "since I must wait for morning to complete the assignment I was given more than a twelvemonth ago, and since we have already established that I cannot thrust you out into the streets, alone and unchaperoned, I have no alternative but to see you tucked away some place safe until my mission is completed."

Brad had not missed that note of panic in her voice when he mentioned getting a room at the inn. She was frightened—and who could blame her?—but this was none of his doing. He had not bid her follow him from the house with a pistol. Her purpose in doing so was still a mystery to him, but whatever bee had gotten into her bonnet, she certainly had not expected to be whisked away, without her consent, for a midnight coach ride to London.

Of course, considering the circumstances, he could not have acted any differently. She had taken him by surprise, and he had reacted in the manner that had kept him alive since he first arrived in the peninsula. With only seconds to decide what was best to do, he had tossed her into the carriage. Now, of course, he wished another solution had occurred to him. Since it had not, he was obliged to make the best of a bad bargain and to do all within his power to right any wrong he may have done her by taking her away with him.

Unfortunately, Miss Rosalind Hinton was not some opera dancer he could put in a hackney and send home, with no one caring that she had spent a number of hours alone with a man who was unrelated to her. She was a gently reared young lady—one in imminent danger of being compromised—and it behooved Brad to do everything he could to insure that both she and her reputation came to no irreparable harm as a result of this night's foolishness.

Of equal importance was his wish to shield himself from being caught in parson's mousetrap. He had no desire to be tied to one woman for life, even one as appealing as the lady opposite him. For that reason, he had thought of nothing else for the past two hours except how to return her safely to Hertfordshire, and he had finally come upon a plan he hoped would serve both the lady and himself.

Once they arrived at the inn, he intended to hire a maidservant to be with Miss Hinton every second—a maid he would instruct to stick to the lady like a plaster. Then, on the morrow, he would see that Miss Hinton, along with her chaperon, was aboard the return coach to Upper Stanton. With any luck at all, she might arrive at Vernon House before her absence was noted. And should she be missed, he felt confident that he could depend upon Lady Sizemore and Sir Miles to keep this unfortunate episode quiet.

"If you are nervous about remaining at the inn until

morning, Miss Hinton, allow me to set your mind at ease. I have no designs upon your virtue."

This was plain speaking, indeed, and Rosalind felt her entire body grow warm at the implication of his words. Though she was relieved to learn that he had no licentious designs upon her, at the same time, some perverse vanity was offended by the implication that she was not desirable enough to tempt a man to try to seduce her.

"I was not nervous, sir, merely—"

Whatever she had hoped to say to persuade him to let her go, the words were lost forever when the coach swerved to the right, slinging the passengers none-too-gently against the sides of the vehicle. Within moments, the driver pulled the horses into a busy inn yard and reined them in. "Whoa, team," he shouted.

When the coach came to a lurching stop before a sprawling three-story half-timbered building, Rosalind peeped out the window to see if she recognized the place. She did not. In the moonlight, the yard and inn appeared clean enough, but if the raucous songs and laughter coming from the taproom were any indication, the innkeeper was not particularly discriminating regarding the social strata of his guests.

Immediately a young ostler in shirtsleeves and leather apron ran to see to the team, unhitching them at an amazing speed then leading them around back to the stables. Meanwhile a second man, this one a bit older, yanked open the door of the coach. "Welcome to the Baited Bear, sir."

As if reciting a litany, he singsonged, "Ye'll find no better inn on the Lunnon road, sir, and that's the truth of it. The beds is well aired, and the food's tasty, and if a gentleman wants a second helping of 'is mutton, the landlord don't turn nasty. And should that gentleman find 'is whistle going dry, there be nothing to fear, for the ale flows the live long night.''

His recitation at an end, the ostler glanced at Rosalind, who had pulled back into the shadows of the coach, her face hid against the squabs. "And if it's privacy yer looking for," he said, not bothering to lower his voice, "this is the place. Won't nobody disturb a gentleman if that's 'is wish.''

"That will do!" the spy said, his tone sharp. "Go on about your business.''

As soon as the ostler stepped away from the coach, Rosalind felt a hand upon her arm. "Miss Hinton," her kidnapper said quietly, "I know you must be concerned, but if you will do as I say, I promise, all will come right.''

She turned to look at the man who was bending close. In that moment, she desperately wanted to believe his promise. But how could this possibly come right? Here she was about to exit the relative security of the coach to enter a place where a certain kind of privacy could be had, no questions asked.

"While I help you to alight," he said, "keep your head down. Once your feet touch the ground, I will put my arm around you and pull you close—''

At her gasp, he paused, biting back a swear word. "This is for your own protection, madam, so I would advise you not to enact me a Cheltenham drama. Do you wish someone to see you and perhaps recognize you?''

Rosalind shook her head.

"Then pay attention. Follow my instructions, and it will go the better for you.''

As soon as she nodded her agreement, he continued. "When I pull you close, bury your face against my shoulder and keep it there. If you wish, you may also pull the lapel of my greatcoat around for even more protection. And whatever you do, say nothing. Understood?"

Rosalind swallowed. "Understood."

He jumped down from the coach, then he turned and held his arms out to Rosalind, lifting her down quickly and with ease. As he had warned, he put his arm around her shoulders and drew her against the hard wall of his chest, holding her fast. With her nose only inches from his neck, she could not avoid breathing in the clean, spicy smell of his shaving soap, and for just a moment the tantalizingly masculine aroma—

Heaven help me! I must be deranged! There was no other explanation for it. The man had kidnapped her, might even be planning to do away with her at his earliest convenience, and she was allowing the fragrance of him to go to her head. Furious at herself for acting like a brainless widgeon, she yanked at the lapel, folding it over to cover her profile; she was grateful when her senses were assaulted by the smell of camphor coming from the long-stored greatcoat.

"We will walk slowly," he said, whispering into her hair. "Ready? Begin."

The ostler approached them again. "Shall I see to your traps, sir?"

"We have none."

The fellow did not exhibit the least surprise at the information. "Very well, sir. Step this way, if you please."

In Rosalind's admittedly limited experience, she had never heard of a respectable inn that would accept the kind of patrons who traveled without luggage, not to mention a lady who wore neither hat nor coat, and was obliged to hide her face in a gentleman's shoulder. Since the ostler did not seem concerned by any of these particulars, she could only assume this was the kind of disreputable place where people sought accommodations for only an hour or so. Mortified to be entering such an establishment, she was content to remain anonymous while her captor greeted the landlord and asked for a room for the entire night.

"And the lady will require the services of a maid," he said.

Surprised, Rosalind peeped out at him with one eye, unable to credit her ears. What kind of kidnapper supplied his victim with a personal servant?

"We don't cater to the carriage trade," their host grumbled. "Them as stops 'ere do for themselves. There be no female servants save the kitchen 'elp and the serving wenches. As for the sculleries, they be abed at this hour, and the wenches 'ave all they can do to keep the tankards filled." He waited for several seconds, his fleshy fingers drumming upon the wooden counter. Then he said, "Wot's it to be? Ye want the room or not? Speak up, for if I'm too long from the taproom, the wenches'll be stealing me hard-earned profits."

"We will take the room."

Rosalind heard the scratch of a quill on paper, then the sound of a key being slapped onto the counter.

"Top o' the stairs. Third door on yer left." With that, the landlord stomped off, presumably returning to the dispensing of ale, leaving his guests to find their way as best they could.

"The lady will require the services of a maid."

Her captor's words echoed through Rosalind's brain all the while they climbed the narrow, uneven stairs and searched the dimly lit corridor for the third door on the left. What did he mean by the request? Not for one moment had she anticipated such unlooked-for consideration.

The thick key scraped in the lock. The door was opened to reveal a small, sparsely furnished bedchamber. Other than the crudely fashioned oak bed, with its faded maroon counterpane, the room boasted nothing more than a rickety washstand, a straight-back chair, and a half-dozen pegs on the walls for hanging clothes.

"I am sorry," he said, the moment the door was closed and locked behind them.

"For what, sir?" The last thing Rosalind had expected to hear from him was an apology. In all truth, this evening had been filled with episodes for which a decent man might feel obliged to beg her pardon; still, she could not hide her surprise that *he* had done so.

"I had hoped to secure a chaperone for you. One who could wait with you for what remained of the night then accompany you back to Hertfordshire on the morrow." He tossed his greatcoat over the back of the chair. "I did not dream there would be no one available. I fear this complicates matters."

His words sounded sincere, confusing Rosalind even more. "Complicates matters in what way?"

He moved across the uncarpeted room, his boots thudding softly on the hard wooden floor. Then he lit the single candle on the washstand. As he stood there, seemingly lost in thought, the flame illuminated his dark blond hair and softened the angular planes of his face, giving him the look of one of the saints in a Michelangelo painting.

"Surely, Miss Hinton, you cannot be unaware that by taking you off as I did, I have compromised your reputation?"

"Compromi—" She paused, for the idea was too

ludicrous for words. "That is the complication that has you worried?"

"Naturally. Never tell me it did not concern you as well."

Rosalind could only stare. "In truth, sir, I was much too concerned for my life."

It was his turn to stare at her. "Your life? Madam, I admit I acted foolishly in tossing you into the carriage and taking you away from Vernon House, but in all honesty I can think of nothing I have said or done to make you fear for your life. Just what sort of man do you think me?"

Without hesitation, Rosalind replied, "I know exactly what you are, sir. You are a French spy."

Chapter Six

"A *French* spy, did you say?"

He stared at her for a moment, shock writ plainly upon his face, then he burst out laughing. The deep, masculine sound boomed inside the small room like a cannon, and for the second time that evening Rosalind knew a desire to box the man's ears.

After a time, he removed a handkerchief from inside his coat and wiped the tears of mirth from his eyes. "A French spy. Madam, where on earth did you get such a corkbrained idea?"

"It was not corkbrained!"

He held up his hand as if to prevent further discussion. "Your pardon, I am sure. If nothing else, that explains why you followed me. As well, it sheds some light upon the very peculiar remark you made while holding that dueling pistol pointed directly at my heart."

"It was not at all peculiar!"

He laughed again. "On the contrary. You said something about being a loyal Englishwoman, and as such, not hesitating to shoot an enemy of your country. Now, of course it makes sense. At the time, however, I thought it mere theatrics."

Rosalind was growing angrier by the minute. How dare he belittle her sense of patriotism. "I daresay you would not have branded it theatrics if I had shot you!"

"No, not then."

"And I might have done so," she continued, "if only the . . ."

When she stopped suddenly, he gave her a quizzical look. "You might have shot me if only the what?"

Suspecting that he would think her a fool, she lifted her chin defiantly. "If there had been a bullet in the pistol."

He stared at her as though he had encountered a lunatic. "You pursued a man you thought an enemy of your country, one you believed capable of murdering you, with an unloaded weapon?"

His incredulity being unanswerable, Rosalind chose to consider the question rhetorical and remained silent.

"Madam," he said, "anyone who acts as you have this night is clearly bereft of their senses and should be kept under lock and key."

Rosalind looked pointedly at the door. "Interesting that you should mention those particular restraints, sir, for I believe that describes my present situation to a nicety."

He looked from the door to her, then he had the grace to avert his gaze from her face. Presently, he reached inside his coat and removed the key, holding it out to her. "You may leave at any moment you wish,

Miss Hinton. I give you my word I shall not attempt to stop you."

When she did not take the key, he caught her hand and placed the cold metal in her palm, closing her fingers around it. "I admit that bringing you here in the first place was an act of total idiocy, for which I offer you my humblest apologies, but not for one instant did I consider you my prisoner."

Brad watched her face while she mentally recapitulated the night's events. Hers was a totally open countenance, one obviously unused to dissembling, and he could read in her eyes the moment she took her share of the blame for their predicament.

"You are not a French spy? You are very sure of this."

"Very sure. Our government has a pact of permanent friendship, for want of a better phrase, with the Portuguese dating from 1386 when the Treaty of Windsor was signed. Because of my command of both French and Portuguese, plus a rather unusual talent for committing facts to memory, I was sent to the peninsula to gather information that might assist our armies in putting a stop to Napoleon's presence in Portugal."

She closed her eyes, as if unable to look at him. "How could I have been so mistaken?"

Obviously not expecting any sort of answer, she walked over and sat down on the edge of the bed where, for a moment, she leaned against the carved oak of the headboard. "You are not the only one guilty of idiocy, sir. This debacle is almost entirely my fault, and to my further embarrassment, I must admit that my actions were predicated on only one fact: that I knew you were not Lieutenant George Ashford. If I had possessed even a degree of sense, I would have revealed that piece of information to Sir Miles and left it with him to seek the full truth of the matter. I had no business following you and interfering with your plans. You have a right to go wherever you wish without answering to me.''

"You are too hard on yourself, Miss Hinton. Though part of what you say is true, I refuse to allow you to take the lion's share of the blame for this night's work.''

He walked over to stand in front of her, his right hand held out in offered friendship. "What say you, ma'am, that we split the dubious honors down the middle and let bygones be bygones?''

After the briefest of hesitation, she placed her hand in his and they shook on it, as though to seal a bargain. "Agreed, sir, if . . .''

"If?'' he repeated.

She blushed again, and with her soft, warm hand in his Brad forgot how angry he had been with her earlier and recalled only how captivating he had thought her when they first met—she with her green eyes and that hint of impishness that had prompted her to tease him about being his fiancée.

"If,'' she continued, easing her hand from his, "you will tell me who you really are.''

"Of course. Within a few hours I shall complete my mission, and at that time all necessity for secrecy will be at an end. Therefore, I shall inform you that my name is Bradford Stone, and that my home is in Sussex. Part of what you were told of me is true, for I was captured by the French in January of this year, after the battle of Corunna.''

"When Sir John Moore was killed, and our army was forced to retreat to the coast?''

"The very time. It was a period of absolute bedlam, and confusion reigned. Because of the resulting chaos, the French soldiers captured those of our troops at the rear of the lines. It was my misfortune to be too close to that line and I was imprisoned alongside many of the men of the gallant Fifty-second Regiment. That is when I met your friend, George Ashford.''

"So you do know the lieutenant.''

"I do. In the six months Ashford and I were in the prison camp together, I came to know and respect him. He is a fine man.''

"Then how—'' She bit her bottom lip as if to stop the question Brad did not blame her for asking.

"How was I repatriated in his place?''

She nodded.

"I cannot tell you with any degree of certainty, for I was ill during the actual exchange, but I believe my coming home had something to do with a debt the lieutenant felt he owed me.''

"What sort of debt?''

He hesitated only a minute, using the interim to walk over to the straight-back chair and pull it out. When he was seated, he said, "Ashford believes I saved his life.''

Her eyebrows lifted in surprise. "And did you?''

"Perhaps. Who can say?''

"I should think *you* could. After all, you were there.''

"True, but being present during life-threatening circumstances does not necessarily insure a clear picture of the events. Everyone involved sees the incident through his—or her—own perspective, and one's emotions, be they fear, anger, or despair, further cloud the perception.''

Her countenance was very serious. "I think I see your point. If you would not think it an impertinence, may I ask you to tell me what happened?''

Brad wanted to refuse, for the memory was still too fresh in his mind and far too painful. On the other hand, he supposed there were those who had a right to know—Sir Miles, definitely, and perhaps this pesky female who had involved herself in his life for all the wrong reasons.

"For you to understand," he said, "you must know that the prison camp was a makeshift affair set up on a few acres of leveled farmland confiscated from a Portuguese farmer just before one reaches the Spanish border. There were several thousand of us prisoners—both British and Portuguese—and only a handful of French soldiers to act as guards. To insure that none of us escaped, the guards made us dig a dry moat around the periphery of the farm. The job took several weeks, for it was a very great ditch, perhaps fifteen feet deep and twenty feet wide, the kind a lone man could not climb out of without assistance."

She said nothing, merely nodded her head, encouraging him to continue.

"One day Ashford come to me with a plan for escape. His Sergeant Major was a mountain of a fellow, amazingly strong, and easily capable of supporting a man upon his shoulders. Ashford thought if the three of us went together, we could scale the bank of the moat. He and I could first stand on the Sergeant Major's shoulders, then once we were out, the two of us would pull him up and over."

"Why did the lieutenant choose you? Were you two particular friends?"

He shook his head. "All he knew of me was that I spoke fluent French and Portuguese."

"Talents of inestimable valuable, I should think, if one hopes to escape across a foreign country."

"Quite. Naturally, I agreed to accompany them. I had valuable information that needed to be delivered to the proper authorities, and I could not escape without help."

"So, the three of you became a team."

"Exactly. Our plans made, we had only to wait for a time when we could hide beneath a cloak of darkness. Such a night came within that very week."

Still sitting on the edge of the bed, Rosalind leaned forward, resting her elbows on her knees and cupping her chin in her hands. Fascination and fear mingled within her as she listened to his story of escape.

"Our descent was easy enough; we just slid down the bank. That part of the plan was accomplished in a matter of seconds. Unfortunately, just as Ashford mounted the Sergeant Major's shoulders, to climb over the top to the other side of the moat, the clouds that had obscured the moon drifted and light flooded the area. At that same moment, the French soldier guarding the area closest to us, just happened to be looking our way."

Rosalind gasped. "Oh, no!"

"The guard was very young, hardly more than a boy, and he was even more surprised to discover us than we were to have been discovered. Even at a distance, I could see that he shook with fear. Possibly because of his fright, coupled with his youth and inexperience, he acted rashly, and without shouting a warning for us to desist and return to the camp, he lifted his rifle and took aim directly at Ashford's back."

"Dear heaven. Never say so!"

"With no time to spare," he continued, "I rushed forward, yelling in French for the guard not to shoot. The lad must have thought I meant him harm, for he shot me instead. At first I could not believe it had actually happened; then, within less time than it takes to say it, searing pain exploded in my shoulder. Odd," he said, in the manner of the athlete who never expects to be felled, "one moment I was standing there gazing with incredulity at the blood gushing from my wound, and the next moment I lost consciousness. I know almost nothing of what happened after that."

The young lady's face filled with compassion. "How horrible for you. For all three of you." Tears glistened in her eyes, and when she blinked, the drops spilled over and coursed down her soft cheeks. "Can you ever forgive me?"

Brad was disconcerted by both the tears and the apology. "What on earth have you to be forgiven for?"

"For adding to your difficulties this evening, and for so grievously misjudging you. I thought you an enemy, when all the time you were a hero."

"No, no. I assure you, madam, I am nothing of the sort."

She used the back of her hand to swipe away the tears. "But you are. Deny it all you wish, but you took the bullet meant for Lieutenant Ashford." She stared at his left shoulder, almost as if she could see the wound. "I quite understand that Ashford would feel he owed you a debt of gratitude, for you saved his life."

They talked for quite some time. The lateness of the hour, plus the forced intimacy of their circumstances, lent itself to uninhibited conversation, and in no time they were speaking freely, like two old friends. Rosalind had made herself comfortable on the bed, with her feet tucked beneath her, and Brad had turned the chair around, straddling it with his arms crossed over the straight back.

"Why did you become a spy?" she asked.

"For the adventure I suppose. At that time my father was still alive, and I had little to occupy me. When a man finds the life of a town beau boring, has no calling for the church or politics, and has no wish to embrace the military life and be forced to kill or mutilate his fellow man, little is left in the way of gentlemanly occupation."

"But spying? Was it not terribly dangerous?"

"At times. Not that you have any right to take me to task, madam, for what you did tonight was not only dangerous but also foolhardy. Following a man you believe to be an enemy, and with an unloaded pistol! The possible repercussions of such an act do not bear thinking of. Why on earth did you do something so rash?"

A hint of a smile played on her lips. "For the adventure," she said, giving him back his own answer. "As an unmarried female," she continued, still parroting his reasons, "I have little interesting to occupy my time. When a woman finds the life of a London ape leader not to her liking, has no calling for charity work or the endless stitching of tapestries, and has no wish to become 'The Maiden Aunt' to her nieces and nephews and be forced to kill or mutilate the tykes, little is left in the way of genteel, ladylike occupation."

At her play upon his words, Brad threw back his head and laughed. "*Mutilate the tykes?* Madam, you positively chill my blood, and I begin to suspect I should fall on my knees and thank the powers that be that you never learned to load a dueling pistol."

She chuckled, pleased at his enjoyment of her humor.

"Is your life in Oxfordshire so lacking in convivial pursuits?"

"Not at all," she replied, "for it is a beautiful county,

with much to recommend it. There are the Cotswolds, the Chilterns, Blenheim Palace, and even Banbury—a prosperous town, with or without the fine lady with rings on her fingers and bells on her toes.

"As for my own town of Whitstock, it is a charming place. In addition to its many fine streams for sport fishing, it boasts a number of genial families, all of whom enjoy partaking of the social life offered in the neighborhood. For the ladies, that means paying visits and being visited in return."

"Dissipation indeed, ma'am. No wonder you and your aunt were traveling to Tunbridge Wells."

"Actually, our trip was got up rather quickly, and though I wished most sincerely to stop at Hertfordshire to call upon Lieutenant Ashford, even that visit was planned primarily to escape drifting into the life I described earlier."

"The one in which you stitch tapestries and mutilate small persons?"

"Exactly. As for the final straw—the one that broke the camel's back, as the saying goes—my sister had decided I could pursue no nobler cause than to wait upon her hand and foot for the final three months of her confinement, and my mother seemed to think I ought to find the occupation a rare treat. Needless to say, I saw the handwriting on the wall—if you will forgive my mixing of metaphors—and fled. While away, I had hoped to think of something a bit more constructive to do with the rest of my life."

"Have you thought of anything?" he asked quietly.

"No. But you will be happy to know I have definitely ruled out spy chasing."

Brad admitted that he was quite glad of her decision to forsake the pursuing of spies, and afterward he suggested that she try to get some sleep. "I will wake you before I leave so that you may lock the door behind me."

Something akin to panic showed in her face. "You will come back, will you not?"

"Of course. I shall not abandon you in this place. I will return as soon as I have spoken to the duke."

Her eyebrows lifted in question. "You do not mean the Duke of York?"

"As a matter of fact, I do. It was the Duke of York who sent me to the peninsula. Why do you ask?"

"Oh, dear," she said. "This is most unfortunate."

"What is?" Foreboding gripped Brad's senses as he watched the lady bite her bottom lip, obviously wishing she had not introduced the subject. "Miss Hinton, if you do not tell me immediately, I shall be tempted to murder you after all."

She did not even bat an eye, no longer afraid of him. "You cannot have known, sir, for you were imprisoned and clearly out of touch with the world, but the Duke of York, after having reorganized the army to its present effectiveness, was obliged to resign as its Commander-in-Chief."

"What!"

"It happened about three months ago." She lowered her gaze. "There was a scandal."

"A military one? I do not believe it. Of what nature was this scandal?"

"It centered upon a person called Mary Anne Clarke."

"The Duke's mistress?"

When she continued to avoid his gaze, he said, "Madam, I realize that ladies are supposed not to know of such things as mistresses, but this is no time for such namby-pamby strictures. I need to know what has occurred.''

"Very well, sir. The Duke of York's mistress was accused of using her influence with him to sell commissions. I understand she made quite a fortune for herself before the truth came to light. When all was exposed, his grace agreed to resign, for the good of the military and the country.''

Brad could not believe this had happened. Now what was he to do? To whom was he to report? His assignment had come directly from the duke.

Knowing that he thought best while moving about, he told the lady he was in need of a long walk. "I will take myself off for a time," he said. "While I am gone, you may have some privacy in which to prepare yourself for bed. Get some sleep if you can.''

"What of you?" she asked. "It is you who have been ill. Do you not need rest as well?''

He shook his head. "I will rest after I know what is best to do." He walked to the door. "I will return directly.''

His hand was on the doorknob when she called him back, the key held out to him. "You may have need of this, Mr. Stone.''

"You are certain?''

She nodded. "I trust you, sir.''

Brad took the key, then he raised her hand to his lips. "Your trust is a gift, ma'am, and I thank you for it.''

He still held her hand, and though she did not pull away, she lowered her gaze. "You are welcome, Mr. Stone.''

"After all we have been through, ma'am, I should be pleased if you would call me Brad.''

At this she looked up at him, and for a moment he was captured by a pair of gentle, green eyes. "Brad," she said softly. It had been a long time since anyone had spoken his name, and hearing it upon her lips sent long-forgotten sensations shooting directly to his nerve ends.

"I shall return within the hour," he said, then he turned and exited the room.

As it turned out, it was almost daylight before he returned. He had walked for a mile or more before finding a coppiced tree upon which to rest in the peaceful quiet of the moonlit night. During that time, his brain had worked as hard as his feet. Not only did he need to decide to whom he should report the findings of his mission, but he also needed to determine what was best to do with Miss Hinton.

The former problem proved easiest to solve. Because he was not an actual member of army intelligence, he decided to go to the War Office rather than to the Horse Guards. General Sir Edward Jamison was at the War Office, and Brad trusted him. That august gentleman would know how to use the information Brad had gathered in Spain and Portugal.

Unfortunately, dealing with the problem of Miss Hinton was not so easy. Each time Brad attempted to concentrate on how he might return her to Hertfordshire with her reputation intact, he was sidetracked by the recollection of those green eyes and that soft voice speaking his name, making him long for something he had never known.

Many were the men in the prison camp who talked incessantly of the women they had left at home—the women they loved. For Brad's part, he had never been in love. In lust, yes. In love, never. If the truth be known, he doubted the emotion existed outside the covers of those maudlin poetry collections and the songs young ladies sang by the dozens at parties.

And yet, when Rosalind Hinton had looked up at him, her eyes had been warm as velvet, her mouth soft and generous, her lips smooth and pliant, and the sight of her had ignited something in his soul as well as in his body.

Not that he meant to do anything about it. He had been attracted to many women in the past—women who understood that lust was lust and nothing more— and he expected to please and be pleased by many more such women in the future, but Rosalind Hinton was not among that number. For good or ill, the lady was under his protection—in the strictest sense of the word—and he meant to return her to her family none the worse for having come to London in his company.

How he was to accomplish that task was the question.

The answer had still not come to him when he noticed a definite lightening of the heavens. The moon was waning, and the faintest trace of pink showed in the distant sky. Soon it would be morning and he could speak with Sir Edward at the War Office. After that, Miss Hinton would be his primary concern.

By the time he retraced his steps and entered the inn, it was late enough for him to hire a horse and gig at the stables. "I will be down within the hour," he told the ostler.

After consuming a breakfast of braised eggs and a muffin, accompanied by a tankard of rich, dark home brew, he went up to the room to leave a note for Miss Hinton, informing her of his destination and the approximate time of his return. She was asleep when he got there, her face turned to the wall.

As he set the note in the chair where she would be certain to find it, he noticed that her pretty yellow dinner dress had been hung on one of the wall pegs, and that her satin slippers lay just beneath the bed, the rounded toes peeping out like the noses of two little inquisitive kittens. One of her arms was outside the faded counterpane, and Brad could see her right shoulder, the soft lawn of her shift leaving most of the ivory skin exposed to the ever-growing dawn light. She had loosened her hair, and it lay like a thick, dark blanket across her pillow.

Unable to stop himself, Brad crossed to the bed for a closer look. She was so lovely in the soft light. So trusting. So completely desirable.

He reached out his hand, his only thought to touch the vibrant curls, but without meaning to, he found himself plunging his fingers into the long, silky strands. Employing a slow, gentle stroke, he combed through the lush tresses, enjoying the sensuous feel of her hair sliding between his fingers.

Reluctantly he withdrew his hand. The lady was too vulnerable. And far too tempting. As he continued to gaze at her, he fancied he could smell the clean fragrance of her skin. He longed to move closer, to test for himself the smoothness of the tantalizing flesh of her bare shoulder.

When desire bid him lean down and discover if her lips were as soft and luscious as they appeared, he forced himself to take a step back, and as he did so, she turned slowly and looked up at him. Her eyes were drowsy with sleep and as innocent as a fawn's. Afraid she would read the longing in his gaze, Brad turned away and strode to the door.

He never once glanced back, so he failed to see the yearning in those innocent, sleep-softened green eyes.

Chapter Seven

Brad did not return to the Baited Bear until well past midday, and by the time he knocked at the chamber door, then fitted the key into the lock, Rosalind had grown quite anxious.

"Brad," she said, the moment he stepped inside the room. "I had begun to think you had forgotten my very existence."

"Oh ye of little faith," he said, smiling like a man who had not a care in the world. "Did you not get my note?"

"Yes, but ..." At sight of him, Rosalind's heart skipped a beat, for he had undergone a miraculous change in appearance. He was dressed in the height of fashion, in a beautifully cut coat of Devonshire brown worn over straw-colored breeches and a waistcoat of palest fawn with a thin gold stripe. The snow white neckcloth was tied with a precision that must have excited envy in the breast of even the most discerning gentlemen of fashion. The breeches fit his form to perfection, revealing his superb fitness, the strength, length, and shape of his muscular legs.

Rosalind was saved from the sin of ogling by his calling her attention to his fawn-colored waistcoat. "The color made me think of you," he said. Since he offered no explanation for this baffling non sequitur, Rosalind merely nodded her approval.

"As my father would say, sir, you look as fine as fivepence."

He made her an exquisite bow. "Madam, you are too kind."

"Actually, what I am is hungry. Ravenously so. At one point, I seriously considered beating upon the chamber door until someone came to set me free. And allow me to inform you, sir, that I would have put my plan into motion had I known you meant to spend the better part of the day at your tailor's, attempting to outshine Mr. Brummell."

Apparently his good humor was impervious to insult, for he smiled, choosing to take her remarks as jest. "I have ordered a meal sent up right away, ma'am, so that is an end to at least one of your complaints. Meanwhile," he added, setting several plainly wrapped packages on the bed, "perhaps you might wish to have a look at the items I purchased on your behalf. I am persuaded you will be pleased to have them in your possession."

Curiosity soon conquered both her feeling of ill-use and her sense of decorum, and Rosalind hastened to untie the strings that secured the packages. When the papers were folded back, she found a blue kerseymere cloak, a small, soft-brimmed hat of blue watered silk trimmed in tiny feathers, wheat-colored kid gloves, and plain jean half boots. The final, and perhaps most surprising package, contained tooth powder and a comb.

Until she lifted out each item and set them one by one upon the bed, Rosalind said nothing. When they were all laid out in a row, she turned to Brad, all her anger and anxiety vanished like the morning mist before the sun. "Thank you, sir. This was most thoughtful of you. Now I can travel without embarrassment."

To her surprise, he looked away, almost as if her words had embarrassed him. After a moment, he cleared his throat. "I have thought of a plan that might work for us."

"Us?"

"Work for you, I should say. 'Tis a way you can explain, to the satisfaction of all, your sudden absence from Hertfordshire."

Rosalind did not think it at all likely that even the truth would be adequate explanation, especially not for her mother and father, but she held her peace, choosing instead to listen politely to his plan.

"It was late morning when I concluded my business at the War Office, and as I—"

"Did that go well, by the way? I could not help but wonder."

"Quite well. General Sir Edward Jamison was most flatteringly pleased to see me, and he declared the information I had gathered to be of prime importance to the permanent removal of French troops from the Iberian Peninsula. As I left his office, a dispatch was being prepared to be delivered to Sir Arthur Wellesley, who returned to Portugal just last month to lead the troops. Sir Edward had the information I gave him included in that dispatch."

"I am pleased to hear it. You must feel such a sense

of accomplishment, not to mention relief, for having completed a long and difficult assignment. Your country owes you a debt of gratitude."

He muttered something noncommittal; then, as if not wishing to give undue importance to his contribution to the war effort, he feigned annoyance. "If it please you, madam, may I now finish relating the story you were so rude as to interrupt?"

Rosalind had difficulty suppressing a giggle. "Your pardon, sir. It was discourteous of me to stop you *in medias res,* as it were. Proceed with your account of your morning. And do not, I pray you, omit a single detail, for you find me positively breathless with eagerness to hear the whole."

"Cut line, Miss Hinton. I know when I am being condescended to."

This time she laughed freely. "Only a very little, I assure you. But, please, do continue. I promise not to interrupt again."

Because she chose to wet her fingertip and use it to cross her heart, the action as unpretentious as that of a child, Brad gave over his pretended anger. "After I concluded my meeting with Sir Edward and went back out into the street, I chanced to see a gray-haired dowager being driven about in an antiquated landau. That was when the plan came to me, for both the carriage and the lady put me in mind of my grandmother."

"How . . . how nice."

"If your puzzled expression is anything to go by, Miss Hinton, I daresay I am being obtuse. I should perhaps inform you that my grandmother often comes to town for the season and remains here until some time in June."

"That is all very nice, and I am sure I wish her every

enjoyment of the season, but I cannot see what this has to do with—"

"If my grandmother is in London at this time, our problem will be solved, for I can take you to her and she will see to it that all the difficulties are worked out."

Rosalind's expression obviously had not relaxed, for Brad reached out and touched her forehead just above the bridge of her nose, using his fingertip to smooth out the slight frown. It was a teasing gesture, and it meant nothing—at least that was what she told herself while she pointedly ignored the tingling sensation that stole up her spine.

Unaware of the havoc he had wreaked upon her senses with just the touch of his fingertip, Brad continued. "I see you have doubts, but believe me, my grandmother is a formidable grand dame. She will know how to win over Lady Sizemore and anyone else who has been told of your disappearance last evening."

Hoping to regain her calm, Rosalind concentrated upon his words. Regrettably, she was unable to share in his enthusiasm, especially if his grandmother was, as he put it, a formidable grand dame.

In Rosalind's experience, such women, though perfectly willing to be amused by the roguish behavior of a personable young gentleman, did not apply that same open-mindedness to young females who flaunted the dictates of propriety. When dealing with members of their own sex, those same grand dames were far more likely to issue a public denouncement. Seldom could those righteous ladies be depended upon to aid the sinner in concealing her transgression.

As it transpired, Rosalind was obliged to keep her misgivings to herself. A knock sounded at the door, announcing the arrival of one of the kitchen maids with the meal Brad had bespoken earlier. While Rosalind turned her back, pretending to study the small grebe feathers curling around the watered silk hat, Brad engaged the servant in small talk to divert her inquisitive glances away from his traveling companion.

After the meal was consumed, he went belowstairs to give Rosalind a few minutes of privacy in which to refresh herself. "I will await you in the inn yard," he said as he exited the room. "You will find me beside the gig I hired to convey us to my grandmother's town house in Cavendish Square."

Not by so much as a batted eyelash did Rosalind reveal her surprise upon hearing the exclusive Mayfair address. Who was Brad's grandmother that she resided in an area peopled by society's wealthiest and most elite citizens? Perhaps more to the point, who—or what—did that make Mr. Bradford Stone?

"Come down when you are ready," he said, breaking in upon her troubled thoughts, "but remember to pull the hood of your cloak well over your face. And no matter what, speak to no one."

The advice was easy to obey, for Rosalind saw no one while she hurried down the steps and out to the waiting gig. Within a matter of moments she was seated beside Brad, who wasted no time in turning the horse and hurrying from the inn yard, leaving the Baited Bear behind them.

The journey into town required no more than a quarter of an hour, and they had reached Marylebone before Rosalind relaxed enough to push aside the hood to her cloak. Because it was not yet the fashionable hour to take the air, those of society who wished to see and be seen were not in evidence. The gig passed only the usual complement of pedestrians, plus a few drays, hackneys, and tradesmen's wagons.

Their progress went unnoticed until Brad turned the horse onto Wigmore then bore right into Cavendish Square. At that time, a youngster perhaps four years old, returning from the park with his nanny, paused to stare openly at the gentleman in the Devonshire brown coat and the lady in blue. Unable to stop herself, Rosalind smiled at the child, but the smile faded quickly enough when Brad reined in the horse before a handsome four-story town house.

Though not one of the so called "great houses" such as Melbourne House, the building was, nevertheless, an admirable example of the kinds of establishments preferred by country gentlemen whose families visited London only for the duration of the season. Simple yet functional, the edifice was fashioned of brown stock brick and embellished with coade stone ornamentation around the door and windows.

A footman must have been on the watch at the front window, for Rosalind's perusal of the architecture had only just reached the iron work of the decorative balconies on the second floor when the entrance door was thrown open and a liveried servant came bounding down the steps.

"Good afternoon, sir," the tall, young footman said politely, going to the horse's head and catching hold of the animal's halter. "It is good to see you again, if you'll pardon my saying so as shouldn't."

"Thank you," Brad said. "Is Lady Browne in residence?"

Lady Browne? Please, let it not be so! A grand dame was one thing; the dowager Lady Browne was something else altogether. How could Rosalind expect help from the widow of a peer?

Rosalind Hinton was the daughter of a respectable gentleman, and as such she felt herself qualified to mingle in all but the most exalted circles. That being true, she was still wise enough to the ways of the world to realize that by society's standards she was a country nobody. Unsure what her reception would be inside the house, she took a deep breath to steady her ever-growing nervousness.

"Her ladyship is at home," the servant replied, "but I cannot say if she is receiving."

"She will receive me," Brad said.

Taking Rosalind's arm, he helped her to alight, then he put his hand beneath her elbow while they climbed the six stairs. It was as well, for Rosalind doubted the ability of her knees to sustain her the entire way without his support.

Her shaking limbs were given further cause to betray her when the butler threw open the door, a wide smile upon his deeply wrinkled face. "Sir!" he said. "What a pleasure to see you again. We have been quite worried for your safety, afraid the Frenchies had got you. Are you well, my lord?"

Rosalind only just stopped herself from groaning. The man she had held at gunpoint—the *French spy*—was a peer of the realm!

Though she supposed she should be thankful the butler had not called him, "Your Grace," at the moment that seemed small consolation. The grand dame would never believe Rosalind had not known of Brad's title. Brad's grandmother was certain to suspect that a country nobody—and a spinster, at that—had seized upon

We'd Like to Invite You to Subscribe to Zebra's Regency Romance Book Club and Give You a Gift of 4 Free Books as Your Introduction! *(Worth $19.96!)*

If you're a Regency lover, imagine the joy of getting 4 FREE Zebra Regency Romances and then the chance to have these lovely stories delivered to your home each month at the lowest prices available! Well, that's our offer to you and here's how you benefit by becoming a Zebra Home Subscription Service subscriber:

- 4 FREE Introductory Regency Romances are delivered to your doorstep
- 4 BRAND NEW Regencies are then delivered each month (usually before they're available in bookstores)
- Subscribers save almost $4.00 every month
- Home delivery is always FREE
- You also receive a FREE monthly newsletter, *Zebra/Pinnacle Romance News* which features author profiles, contests, subscriber benefits, book previews and more
- No risks or obligations...in other words you can cancel whenever you wish with no questions asked

Join the thousands of readers who enjoy the savings and convenience offered to Regency Romance subscribers. After your initial introductory shipment, you receive 4 brand-new Zebra Regency Romances each month to examine for 10 days. Then, if you decide to keep the books, you'll pay the preferred subscriber's price of just $4.00 per title. That's only $16.00 for all 4 books and there's never an extra charge for shipping and handling.

It's a no-lose proposition, so return the FREE BOOK CERTIFICATE today!

AFFIX
STAMP
HERE

ZEBRA HOME SUBSCRIPTION SERVICE, INC.

120 BRIGHTON ROAD

P.O. BOX 5214

CLIFTON, NEW JERSEY 07015-5214

a golden opportunity and staged the kidnapping in order to compromise her grandson.

Brad made some sort of reply to the butler's question about his health, then he placed his hand upon the old man's shoulder. "It is good to see you again, old friend."

If possible, the servant's smile grew even wider, and a suspicion of moisture showed in his eyes. "Her ladyship will be so pleased to know that you are home at last. She is in her sitting room, my lord. Allow me to show you up."

"Do not trouble yourself, Winthrop. I will show myself up. Meanwhile," Brad added, turning to include Rosalind in the conversation, "since I fully expect my grandmother to wish a private moment in which to rake me over the coals for my continued absence, I believe Miss Hinton might prefer to wait in the library until the smoke of battle has cleared."

The butler nodded politely to Rosalind. "Perhaps Miss would enjoy a cup of tea?"

"The very thing." Brad gave the old man's shoulder another squeeze before turning to Rosalind once again. "Winthrop will see to your comfort, Miss Hinton, then as soon as my grandmother has time to compose herself, I will return for you."

Taking the narrow, straight stairs two at a time, Brad made his way up to the second floor. Upon entering the sitting room, he found the diminutive, silver-haired lady immaculately attired in a carriage dress of dusty rose, standing before a window that offered a view of the small, walled garden at the rear of the house. Her back was to the door, so she did not immediately notice her visitor. Thinking to gain her attention, Brad cleared his throat.

"Yes? What is it, Winthrop? If that is Mrs. Fitzpatrick

and her sister come to call, be so good as to tell them to—"

"To go to the devil," Brad finished for her, "for my grandson is home from the wars."

The lady turned slowly, her delicate-boned face wreathed in smiles. "Bradford," she said, the slight tremolo in her voice betraying her mixed joy and relief at seeing him, "you are home at last."

When she opened her arms wide, Brad crossed the room; a few long strides were all that was necessary to put him within her reach. At first he bent down, allowing her to embrace him as she wished; then, giving in to impulse, he caught her up in a bone-crushing hug and lifted her off the floor, swinging her around and around until she cried out in protest.

"Set me down, you great lout! Has a year's absence taught you no respect for your elders?"

"None whatsoever, my one-and-only love. Would you have me go away again and see if I can find someone to teach me manners?"

"No, my boy. I would have you no place but here." She put her hands on either side of his face, gazing into his countenance as if to convince herself that he was truly before her. "I have prayed for this moment, and I would not spurn an answered prayer."

"You were ever a wise woman."

"And you, sir, were ever a silver-tongued devil."

She kissed him on both cheeks then pushed him away. "Now, as your grandfather was used to say, 'open your budget.' What trouble have you gotten yourself into this time?"

Brad placed his hand over his heart as if wounded. "Trouble? Me? Grandmother, you cut me to the very soul. I have only just returned from foreign lands, and

I came here straightaway for no other purpose than to greet the person dearest to me in all the world."

She raised her hand, motioning him to silence. "Do not attempt to play me off with one of your taradiddles, you rascal, for I am not to be cozened. I know you too well." She pointed to a gold brocade-covered chair, the only one in the room not pared down for a lady her size. "Now sit down over there and tell me the whole, leaving nothing out."

The dowager Lady Browne heard her grandson's edited account of his imprisonment and repatriation with only the slightest trembling of her lips. As was her way, she remained silent through the entire story, her hands folded in her lap. He related his feelings upon waking at Vernon House and discovering he had been sent home under another man's name. Only when he got to the part about the arrival of the hired coach, and his precipitous kidnapping of Miss Rosalind Hinton, did her ladyship so much as raise an eyebrow.

"And that," he concluded, after giving her a quite sketchy account of his visit to the War Office, "is when I thought to bring Miss Hinton to you. I assured her that you would know what was best to do to preserve her reputation."

"Of course I know what to do," Lady Browne said finally, "and so, I wager, do you. You have kidnapped this young person and removed her from the protection of her home and family. Such action leaves you with no recourse, my boy. You must marry the girl."

Chapter Eight

"Marriage is out of the question," Brad said. "It is the one thing I will not do."

Brad could not believe his grandmother had suggested such a thing. Not Millicent Browne! His grandparents had been devotedly, passionately in love with one another for forty years. Brad had decided while still a lad that he would never marry unless he found a woman he could love as his grandfather had loved his Milly. "No," he repeated, "I want no part of a marriage of convenience. There must be some other way to satisfy the conventions."

Her ladyship raised a questioning eyebrow. "Is the young person so ineligible, then?"

Brad shook his head. "Not at all. Her father is a gentleman, and her connections, if not exalted, are at least respectable."

"But you find her manners unrefined. Is that the difficulty?"

" 'Certainly not. Rosali—I mean Miss Hinton's— manners are pleasing and unaffected. Now that I think of it, I am persuaded that you and she would get along like old friends in no time at all."

"Would we now? If that is true, then I must assume she is not one of those females with more hair than wit, for you know I cannot abide empty-headed chatter. And if I remember correctly, neither can you. A ninnyhammer would drive a man like you to distraction."

For some reason, Brad found the conversation irritating. "Miss Hinton is no ninnyhammer. She is an educated and intelligent woman."

He did not miss the speculative look in the older lady's eyes. "How very interesting," she said. "I surmise, then, that your objection to the young lady is based solely upon her physical attributes. Is she what you young people call an antidote? I assume you find her terribly unhandsome."

"Not in the least! And I would appreciate it, Grandmother, if you would not credit me with opinions I do not hold. Rosalind Hinton is one of the most beautiful women I have ever seen."

"As comely as all that?"

"Quite. And before you question her temper, ma'am, allow me to inform you that hers is a most amiable nature."

Brad had forgotten how exasperating his grandmother could be when she got an idea into her head. Only let her decide a thing needed doing, and she was like a dog gnawing at a bone—chomp, chomp, chomp until she got her way.

"If you are searching for faults in Miss Hinton," he said, "you might just as well save yourself the task, for the only one I have discovered is her tendency toward rash behavior. Though, from something she let slip last evening, I am convinced she was goaded into the initial imprudence by a family whose members have no notion how to appreciate her as she deserves."

If her ladyship drew any conclusions from this last observation, she chose to keep them to herself.

"Now let me see if I have heard you correctly, my boy." She lifted her hand, spread her fingers, then touched them one at a time as she counted off the salient points. "You tell me the young lady is well-bred, educated, and has a pleasant disposition. Furthermore, by your own admission, she is beautiful. The most beautiful woman you have ever beheld, I think you said. Have I the right of it?"

Brad made no reply, but his countenance was decidedly stormy and angry lights showed in his blue eyes.

"Well," his grandmother continued, looking meaningfully at the fingers she had used to tick off the score, "one can certainly understand why you would object to marrying such a person. I marvel, my boy, that you were able to tolerate her for as long as you did."

When Brad entered the book-lined room some twenty minutes later and bid Rosalind leave the red leather wing chair and come with him to meet Lady Browne, the stubborn set of his chin robbed Rosalind of what little confidence she had left. His unyielding rigidity, coupled with an apparent wish not to communicate, did not bode well for the coming interview.

What in heaven's name had his grandmother said to him? From his manner, it seemed likely the grand dame had objected to his bringing Rosalind to her home. Had she rung a peal over him? Had she refused outright to lend her assistance?

Rosalind wished they had never come here. For her part, she was quite willing to turn around that instant and exit with all haste, taking her chances that the world and her family would forgive and forget the fact that she had been thoroughly compromised. One word from the man beside her, and she would lift her skirts and run from the premises.

She received no such word, so once they reached the first landing, she slipped her hand into Brad's, needing the support of his touch. At first he stiffened, but after only a moment, his fingers curled around hers, warm and reassuring. "Relax," he said softly. "She will not eat you."

"How can you be sure?"

He looked down at her then, and for the first time since coming to fetch her, he smiled. "Trust me on this, my grandmother will not be hungry. Not after having eaten me for nuncheon."

Rosalind had only just realized the significance of his words when he pushed open a door and ushered her inside a handsome room fitted out in white and gold. Like the furniture, the lady who held out her hand was smaller than average, but striking, with an underlying substantialness about her that belied her delicate appearance.

"Miss Hinton," she said, giving Rosalind's hand a firm squeeze, "welcome to my home."

"Thank you, Lady Browne. I realize this is an unconscionable imposition, but—"

"Pish and tosh, my dear young lady, 'tis no imposition at all. I am always delighted to meet any of my grandson's friends." She cast a meaningful look at that gentleman.

"You may leave us now, Bradford, for I cannot think your particular expertise is needed."

"Grandmother, I—"

"Go. You mentioned something about needing information on sailing schedules from Portsmouth. See to it now, if you please. Have no fear, Miss Hinton and I will discuss nothing you would wish to hear."

She turned to Rosalind and bid her be seated beside her on the gold-trimmed white settee. "The first order of business, my dear, is to put our heads together to compose a letter to your aunt, one I shall have my footman deliver this very day."

Feeling totally out of her depth, Rosalind turned to look at Brad, who stood at the door, having ignored his grandmother's attempts to send him away.

"In the missive," her ladyship continued, "we will explain that I sent you an unexpected invitation for a visit, and in my haste I couched it in such ambiguous language that you deemed it necessary to come away immediately. Once the explanation is completed, we will beg your aunt—Lady Sizemore, is it?—to join us here in town as soon as she can take leave of her host at Vernon House."

Lady Browne did not look at the scowling gentleman who continued to stand beside the door, but at Rosalind. "What say you to that scheme, my dear Miss Hinton? Will it serve, do you think?"

"Of course, ma'am." Actually, Rosalind had heard little past the information that Brad meant to inquire about sailing schedules. Sailing where? Surely he had not accepted another assignment. Not so soon after his return. He had not had ample time to recover fully from his injury.

Heedless of the fact that Lady Browne was speaking

to her, Rosalind looked again toward the door, her gaze meeting Brad's. "Why do you need to know sailing schedules?"

Because she looked directly at the lady's grandson, Rosalind failed to see the interest reflected in his grandmother's eyes. The mutinous look on Brad's face was impossible to miss, however. He had the appearance of a cornered animal about to bolt, and when he did not answer her, she felt the heat of embarrassment rush to her face. "Forgive me," she said. "I had no right to ask such an impertinent question. What you do, and when you do it, are no concerns of mine."

"On the contrary," Lady Browne said, "call me old-fashioned if you will, but I believe a fiancée has every right to know the plans of her intended."

Fiancée! For several moments, her ladyship's words knocked at Rosalind's forehead, seeking admittance to her brain. Unfortunately, her brain, though agreeable to accepting the words, quite adamantly refused to acknowledge their significance. *Fiancée? What fiancée? Brad never mentioned any such person.*

Nor did he mention the word now. Instead, he gave his grandmother a look that said, "Now you have done it!" The look effectively passed and received, he turned and exited the room, closing the door none too gently behind him.

If his grandmother was at all intimidated by his mood or his action, she gave no indication of it. "Well, now," she said, "that was surly behavior from one's intended."

There, she had said that word again, and this time Rosalind could not deny the implication. Embarrassment traveled a heated route up her neck into her face.

"Surly, indeed," Lady Browne repeated. "What must you be thinking of him, my dear?"

Rosalind's brain was in too much of a whirl to allow for coherent thinking. "My thoughts are of no moment, ma'am. What matters is what *you* must be thinking. Or, perhaps, concluding is a better word, for it occurs to me that you may be under the impression that Brad and I are engaged. If so, allow me to disabuse you of that notion."

Her earlier embarrassment was nothing to what she felt at the moment, speaking so bluntly about such an intimate topic. Still, it had to be done. "There is no understanding between Lord Stone and me, nor even any serious attachment. We are but two people who, through a series of misunderstandings, were thrown together for a few days."

"Are you telling me, Miss Hinton, that you have no feelings for my grandson?"

Rosalind closed her eyes, hoping to conceal those disturbing emotions she had not allowed herself to examine before. "The question is irrelevant, ma'am."

"Not to me. I find it imminently relevant, and I should very much like to hear the answer. My grandson is all the family I have left in this world, and his happiness is of great concern to me. So, my dear, let us have no more evasions and roundaboutations. Do you love him?"

"Love him? I do not even know him. I met him less than a week ago, and for most of that time our acquaintance has been far from convivial."

As if to substantiate her assertion, she said, "Just yesterday I believed him to be a French spy, and when I threatened to shoot him, he became so angry at me he tossed me into a moving coach. I ask you, ma'am, does that sound like lover-like behavior?"

To Rosalind's surprise, Lady Browne chuckled, as though pleased by what she had heard so far. "The entire first month his grandfather and I knew each other, we were at daggers drawn, and ours turned out to be a true love match. Forty years we were together, and every year happier than the one before it."

"But, ma'am, there can be no comparison between you and Lord Browne and Brad and me."

"I cannot agree. Bradford is very like his grandfather, who was a complete rogue."

She paused for a moment, as though recalling the man she had loved for almost half a century. "My Harold was the perfect man for me, though my papa did everything he could to separate us." She laughed again, obviously recalling some incident from the past. "Harold's lineage was impeccable. Unfortunately, the same could not be said for his reputation with the ladies. Loving only one woman, and being faithful to her for life, had never figured into his plans."

Interested in spite of herself, Rosalind said, "What changed his philosophy?"

"Me." The diminutive lady smiled rather smugly. "I changed his philosophy. When he fell in love with me, he wanted no one else. For forty years, we were inseparable, needing no one else, wanting no one else save each other."

She closed her eyes for a moment; then, as if she had returned those memories to that private place where they usually resided, she sighed. Looking up at Rosalind, she said, "I told you Bradford was like his grandfather."

"You did, ma'am."

"What I did not say was that you, my dear, remind me of me."

"But, ma'am, I—"

"Shh," she said, "do not waste my time with senseless denial. I am an old lady, and I find dissimulation tiring in the extreme. I can see that you and my grandson will deal extremely well together, and it remains only for a date to be agreed upon before we send the announcement of your engagement to *The Times.*"

This was all happening much too fast for Rosalind. "Lady Browne," she said, her tone brooking no refusal, "though I should not wish to be rude, I must insist that you hear me out. No matter what my feelings for Lord Stone, or how well suited you believe your grandson and me to be, the fact remains that he does not wish to marry me."

"He did not at first," she said, waving aside the objection as though it was of little import, "I readily admit that. But after we talked, and I explained to him the slights a compromised woman is often obliged to endure, the outright ostracism, in some instances, he finally came around."

"He—he came around!"

The words were like a blow to Rosalind's pride, and to her heart. She recalled the stubborn set of Brad's chin when he had fetched her from the library, then his coolness and quiet anger as they climbed the stairs. No wonder he had reminded her of a condemned man, that must have been exactly how he felt.

Unable to sit still another minute, Rosalind rose from the settee and walked over to the window. Pushing aside the lace curtains, she stared fixedly down at the small garden without seeing any of its slightly unkempt beauty.

In time, she turned back to look at the silver-haired

lady who sat quietly, her dainty hands folded serenely in her lap. "Lady Browne," she said, "I appreciate your suggestion about the letter, and I gratefully accept the offer. I believe that sending for my aunt will convince the inquisitive that my abrupt departure from Vernon House was the result of an invitation from you. The letter, coupled with my aunt's subsequent arrival here at your town house, should be more than sufficient to rectify any damage done to my reputation."

She was obliged to take a deep breath before continuing. "Therefore, though I thank you for your further concern on my behalf, I find I cannot—nay, I will not—marry your grandson."

"Will not? But, my dear, you must."

"Please, ma'am, say no more upon the subject. I may be a spinster, and one well past her hopes of an advantageous marriage, but I want no part of a reluctant husband."

Having said this, she walked over and opened the door, pausing just beyond the threshold. "And," she added, a hint of tears clogging her throat, "you may inform your grandson that he is free to come and go as he pleases without any further question from me." Rosalind lifted her chin and squared her shoulders, regaining some of her pride. "For his information, and yours, ma'am, I have no wish to share my life with a man who finally came around."

What her ladyship would or would not inform her grandson remained to be seen. To the skinny, middle-aged lady's maid who entered the room once the visitor had rushed past her and hurried down the stairs, she said, "I have good news, Clotilde."

"Vraiment, m'lady?"

"Truly," she replied, "for I believe my grandson has brought me the very young lady who will ensure his future happiness."

Clotilde, a true romantic, sighed. *"C'est bon,* m'lady."

"Yes," her ladyship agreed. "Unfortunately, they are both behaving most obstinately. It remains for you and me to put our heads together to see how a marriage between them is to be achieved."

Rosalind had descended the stairs in rather unseemly haste. She returned to the library and the relative privacy of one of the red leather wing chairs, chiefly because she had no place else to go. In due time, however, a female servant, rail thin and wearing the small, frilly cap and apron of a lady's maid appeared at the door. After she curtsied respectfully, she introduced herself.

"I am Clotilde, *mademoiselle,* and I have come to show you to your bedchamber. If you will please to follow me."

Happy to know she would finally have a place where she might find a moment's real privacy in which to smooth balm upon her wounded feelings, she followed the woman up to the second landing where the guest bedchambers were located.

"Lady Browne informs me, *mademoiselle,* that your luggage has been delayed and will not be here until tomorrow when your aunt arrives. For this reason, I have taken the liberty of placing a few necessary items in your *chambre* à *coucher.* Once you have disrobed, I will see to it that the dress you are wearing is pressed and ready in time for the evening meal."

At that moment, the mere idea of partaking of a

meal, never mind that it was still two hours away, caused Rosalind's stomach to teeter, making her feel decidedly ill. She was searching for some plausible excuse to absent herself from dinner when Clotilde opened the door and ushered her into the rear bedchamber, putting thoughts of excuses from her mind.

It was a pretty room, and very feminine, done in various shades of green—from the dark verdigris of the carpet to the palest jasper of the bed hangings. As if in harmony with the decor, across the foot of the bed lay an exquisitely sewn wrapper of sea green tiffany silk trimmed in blond lace.

Unable to resist, Rosalind lifted one of the sleeves to examine the minute stitches. They were perfection, as was the delicate, spider-web transparency of the tiffany.

"I—I could not possibly borrow anything so lovely. Please thank Lady Browne, but tell her I—"

"The wrapper is mine, *mademoiselle*, fashioned by my own hands, and I should like very much to see it worn by a young lady like you, you with your pretty bosoms and your lovely dark hair. *Moi*, I had the pretty bosoms when I was younger. Now," she said, shrugging her shoulders in a manner that was pure Gaelic, "time has taken the color from my hair and the fullness from my figure." She sighed. *"C'est la vie."*

While she talked, the woman turned Rosalind around and began to undo the tiny buttons at the back of the jonquil dinner dress. "If *mademoiselle* would like it," she continued, "I should be pleased to fashion all the lingerie for the wedding trousseau."

She kissed her fingers then sighed as if in ecstasy. "The soft silks. The gossamer sheer lawns. The delicate laces. I make them all obey my needle. For you, *mademoiselle*, I shall sew a dozen wrappers, each one more beautiful, more alluring than the one before it. When *monsieur la baron* sees you, he will find you so irresistible he will not be able to—"

"You have been misinformed!"

Rosalind was not certain which embarrassed her most, the image of Brad gazing at her clothed in nothing but a gossamer wrapper and finding her irresistible, or the fact that she had to admit to this romantic-minded stranger that she would have no need for the lovely, intimate items. Having reached the age of five and twenty, with no offers for her hand, she would probably never need them. "I shall not be wanting a trousseau, Clotilde. Nonetheless, I . . . I thank you for your kind offer."

The servant *tsk tsked*. "The English young ladies, they are so very modest." She began lifting Rosalind's dress up over her head. "We shall speak again when *mademoiselle* feels less shy."

Not knowing how to respond to the maid's assumption that the subject was still open to discussion, Rosalind let the matter rest, thankful that Clotilde said no more for the moment. Silently the lady's maid unfastened Rosalind's hair and brushed it out, then asked if she would like the covers of the bed turned back so she might have a nap before dinner.

"Thank you, no. I believe I would prefer to enjoy the view from the window."

"As you wish, *mademoiselle*. I will return in time to help you dress for dinner."

Rosalind took the course of least resistance and did not tell the woman that she wanted no part of the meal. Instead, while still hoping some plausible excuse for

remaining abovestairs might occur to her, she availed
herself of the upholstered window seat, curling up with
her bare feet tucked beneath her and her back flush
against the cool wall of the embrasure. While she gazed
down at the charmingly untamed garden below, she let
her mind wander, hoping the solitude and quiet might
help her rid her thoughts of the many *what ifs* that had
plagued her since her conversation with Lady Browne.

What if she and Brad were engaged? What if his grandmother was in the right of it and they would deal
extremely well together? Most importantly, what if he
had readily agreed to an engagement? If that had been
the case, what would Rosalind have done?

An hour or so later, still unable to answer those unanswerable questions, she gave herself up to the beauty
of the westering sun. Breathtaking strokes of orange,
blue, and purple painted the sky, while shafts of light
pierced the leaded windowpanes, casting soft rainbow
colors upon her lap and upon the carpet beyond the
embrasure.

Rosalind was enjoying the play of light upon the sea
green tiffany silk of the borrowed wrapper when a knock
sounded at the bedchamber door. Thinking it was Clotilde, returned with her dress, Rosalind called out permission to enter. To her surprise, when the door
opened, the person who paused just outside the threshold was not the lady's maid but Brad. He had changed
into a dark blue dinner coat worn over a silver-striped
waistcoat, and he looked so handsome he stole her
breath away.

"May I speak with you?" he asked.

In her embarrassment at having been caught *en dishabille,* Rosalind immediately swung her feet to the ground

and stood. Unfortunately, her legs had been tucked
beneath her for too long and they had gone to sleep.
Now they threatened to give way beneath her. Afraid
she might topple over if she crossed the room, she
remained before the window, placing her hand against
the wall to maintain her balance. "Please," she said,
ignoring the thousands of pinpricks running up her
ankles, "come in."

Brad stepped just inside the room, being careful to
leave the door wide open for propriety's sake. While
dressing, he had downed a brandy, or perhaps it had
been two, to fortify himself for the task of proposing
marriage. He had hoped to complete the job with as
much dignity and gentlemanliness as possible, impress-
ing upon Rosalind the necessity for marriage while
being honest about his feelings. He liked her, quite a
bit, actually, far too much to misrepresent the situation.
He wanted no misunderstandings. Though he was willing to do the right thing, he wanted it understood theirs
would not be a love match.

To his dismay, his carefully planned speech and all
those admirable goals were swept completely from his
mind by the sight of Rosalind Hinton as she stood before
the embrasure.

Once again her glorious, silken hair tumbled all about
her shoulders, but it was that other silk—a sea green,
gauzy kind of fabric—that caught his attention. Shafts
of innocent light beamed through the window behind
her; unfortunately, they filtered not nearly so innocently
through her loose-flowing wrapper, revealing the slim-
ness of her waist, the feminine curve of her hips, and
just the hint of her slender, tantalizing thighs.

"Rosalind, I—" He paused, for his mind refused to
cooperate with his voice. Words would not come as he

continued to stare at the beautiful picture she made—
a picture no man could ignore.

"Come in," she said again.

"No. No, I should not have come at all. I see that
now. I . . . we cannot speak here. I will wait for you in
the library."

Turn, Brad told himself. *Turn and walk out the door.*

It was good advice. Excellent advice. But he did not
heed it. Instead, he took one step forward, hoping Rosalind would do likewise. He waited, his heart pounding
like a military drum, willing her to move away from the
window, unnerved by his reaction to the sight of her.
Unnerved by his inability to look away.

She was totally unaware that standing as she was, the
light penetrated the gauzy material, revealing the shape
of her, allowing him to look his fill—no, not his fill!
He cursed himself for gawking like some adolescent
schoolboy; then he cursed himself again for standing
there, willing her to come closer.

Praise heaven, she did not!

After what seemed an eternity, he remembered that
he was reputed to be a gentleman. Though the man in
him shouted at him to cross the room and take the
beautiful creature in his arms, the gentleman in him
whispered that he should leave. The gentleman finally
won out. Without another word, he turned and exited
the room, closing the door very carefully behind him.
Only when he was safely outside at the top of the staircase, his hand upon the newel post, did he breathe
again.

"Damnation," he muttered.

He drew a deep, measured breath, trusting it to steady
his emotions, relying upon it to cool his overheated

body. The ploy did not work. He still wanted to return to her room to . . .

"Damnation," he said again, then he bounded down the stairs two at a time while he still had the willpower to do so.

Chapter Nine

Rosalind stood very still, watching Brad close the door behind him, the action deliberate, quiet. Something had happened here. She was not at all certain what it was, but it had left her trembling from head to toe, and more aware of her femininity than she had ever been before. As well, it had made her wonder if she had been wrong in her earlier assessment of Brad's feelings toward her. Perhaps he was not so opposed to an alliance between them as she had thought. And if *he* was not, then what of her own feelings? Had she, perhaps, been a bit too hasty in her resolve not to wed?

Brad had asked if he could speak with her, then he had stepped inside the room and stopped. He had said almost nothing, however; he had merely looked at her. The expression on his face had been unreadable, but gone was the seductive smile so often in evidence—a smile she felt certain he had perfected on dozens, perhaps hundreds, of willing females. In its place there was a look in his eyes, a look that sent tingling sensations across the surface of Rosalind's skin. To her dismay, those sensations had mesmerized her, eventually overcoming her inhibitions to such a degree that she would have gone to him. But the pinpricks in her ankles had prevented her from taking even one step in his direction.

Brad had said he would wait for her in the library, and eager to join him, to continue what had begun in her bedchamber, she began stamping her feet in a frenzied sort of jig until complete feeling returned to her limbs. Fortunately, since Rosalind would be obliged to dress before she went belowstairs, the lady's maid chose that moment to scratch at the door, then enter the bedchamber, the freshly pressed jonquil lustring over her arm.

"Mademoiselle," she greeted.

"Clotilde, you are come at last. Thank you. Now, if you will, please help me to dress, for Lord Stone is waiting for me."

Taking her cue from the excited young lady, the romantic-minded servant rushed forward, a smile upon her face. *"Mais oui!* Not to worry, *mademoiselle,* for I shall have you ready *tout de suite."*

Her toilette completed at last, Rosalind descended the stairs, confident that she appeared to advantage. Her dress was neat and stylish, and her hair was arranged in a most becoming twist atop her head, with wispy curls of varying lengths framing her face and accenting the nape of her neck.

If butterflies performed a spirited dance inside her, it was no wonder. Some primal feminine instinct convinced Rosalind that after those charged moments in her bedchamber, this would be a momentous meeting, and the closer she came to the library and Brad, the more fanciful became her expectations.

When she entered the book-lined room, with its leather wing chairs and its red and gold patterned Axminster carpet, the cool masculine furnishings had been warmed by the light from two candelabra, one reposing upon the teakwood writing desk, the other placed on the mantel beside a brass carriage clock. To Rosalind's disappointment, more than candlelight was needed to warm the cool masculinity of the tall, handsome man who stood before the partially opened French windows.

For the briefest of moments, when Brad first turned to greet her, a spark had shone in his eyes, assuring Rosalind that Clotilde's efforts with her dress and hair had succeeded admirably. In the next instant, however, that spark was gone.

As if calling himself to attention, so that some onerous task might be got through as quickly and painlessly as possible, Brad donned the polite expression of a welcoming host. Though he smiled and bid her be seated, his manner quite gentlemanly, asking if she would like a glass of sherry, he appeared stiff, uncomfortable with himself and the situation.

His first remarks—whatever they were—were wasted on Rosalind, for she suffered from frustration too intense to allow for polite small talk. Drat this man and his good manners! She had not hurried through her toilette and rushed down the stairs to the library to be hosted!

She had come down seeking the man who had stood in her bedchamber, looking at her in a way that robbed her of sensible thought, all but caressing her with his eyes. This man before her was not the man who had gazed at her with desire—she would call it what it was—less than an hour ago.

She sought that man!

Or if not him, at least let her find the friend who had sat with her in that sparse little room at the Baited Bear, chatting companionably into the wee hours of the morning. Where was that person?

At the very least, she would call for a return of the smiling rogue she had suspected of being a French spy—him with his intense blue eyes and his animal magnetism. She preferred even that rascal to the man who stood before her now.

This man reminded her of Lady Browne's grandson—the one who had *finally come around.*

"Miss Hinton. Rosalind," he amended, taking a deep breath in the manner of one of those mythical warriors who girded up their loins before marching into battle, "I think you cannot be unaware of my reason for seeking this interview."

His words were stilted, correct, and beneath them Rosalind heard a hint of resentment. She closed her eyes, not wanting him to witness the surrender of her foolish expectations. In her own way she had been as romantic-minded as Clotilde: believing the unlikely, embracing the implausible.

Please, she begged heaven, *let me get through this with a modicum of dignity, with my foolish expectations unexposed. Do not let me appear in his eyes like some love-starved spinster willing to take any offer of marriage, even if the offer is made under duress.*

"Well?" he said, the word intruding upon Rosalind's inner conflict, "may I know your answer?"

Heaven help her! She had not even heard what might

well be her only proposal. "Forgive me, sir, but I . . . I seem to have been woolgathering."

"Woolgathering!" His face was almost comical in its incredulity. "Damnation, woman. Do you tell me you have not heard a word I said? Am I to be obliged to say it all again?"

If he had been less angry, Rosalind might have been more courteous. As it was, his anger sparked hers. "I will thank you not to use that tone with me, sir! As for your repeating that which I failed to hear, the decision is quite up to you. It was *you* who requested this interview, as you put it, and since it was none of *my* doing, you may speak or remain silent. Please yourself upon the matter."

"Blast it all, Rosalind! You know we—"

"I warned you not to rail at me," she said, rising from the chair, grateful for the opportunity to quit the room. "For my part, this conversation is now at an end. I will return later when your grandmother comes down. Perhaps her presence will act as a restraint upon your ill manners."

"No! Wait. Please. Forgive me," he said, the words sounding sincere.

Rosalind had already taken several steps toward the door, but hearing his apology, she stopped and turned to look at him. In his frustration, he had run his hand through his hair, mussing it and causing one dark blond lock to fall across his forehead. The fallen lock reminded her of the first time she had ever seen him, when he had been ill and delirious with fever. She had felt compassion for him at that time.

Of course, compassion had soon turned to suspicion—with disastrous results—but when she had learned the full story of his experience on the peninsula, suspicion had finally given way to admiration. Imprisoned by the French, then wounded while saving the life of another, Brad Stone had shown himself to be a hero. In all fairness, his offering for her tonight, if not a heroic act, was certainly the honorable thing to do—the kind of thing he would do.

No matter how she disliked the idea of a coerced proposal, Rosalind was obliged to admit that Brad was trying to act in a gentlemanly manner.

"Please," he said again. "Will you forgive me?"

When she hesitated, he crossed the room to stand beside her, catching her hand in his. "We really do need to talk."

"I am persuaded, sir, that we would be better served to forget the conversation entirely, but if you must have an answer, let me say it now and have done."

"Then you did hear my question?"

She shook her head. "I did not, but I can imagine what you said. I told your grandmother my feelings on the matter, and now I will tell you. I hope that will be an end to it." She paused, obliged to draw a calming breath. "Though I am not unmindful, sir, of the honor you have bestowed upon me by the offer of your hand, I find I must refuse. I thank you, but I do not wish to be wed."

Rosalind did not miss the initial look of relief that flashed through his eyes, though he covered it quickly with one of polite regret. "Are you quite certain?" he said, giving her an opportunity to reconsider her refusal. When she shook her head, he smiled, and it was as if the Brad Stone she knew suddenly returned.

Squeezing her hand, he said, "Actually, ma'am, if I had been obliged to wed, I can think of no one I would rather be leg-shackled to than you."

Upon hearing the cant expression, she gave him a quelling look. "A rare compliment indeed, sir. I hope you will not take it amiss if I do not have it inscribed upon my gravestone."

"Ouch!" he said, laughter quite near the surface. "Madam, your sarcasm skewers me to the core."

"Good," she replied. "You will be the better for a good skewering. Rascals such as you need to be wounded every now and then. It adds just a hint of humility to their overweening arrogance."

This time he laughed aloud. "Skewered anew! I am wounded, if not wed."

"Not wed to me, in any event."

He still held her hand, and now he lifted it, placing his own over hers. "I shall accept your refusal as final, but in doing so, I wish to add that I should be bereft if this incident should come between us and we were no longer friends."

Rosalind said nothing, far too caught up in the sensation of her hand captured by both of his, warmed by the feel of his slightly callused flesh surrounding hers.

"Friends?" he asked, the word spoken softly.

"Yes," she replied.

He did not release her hand, but stood very still, gazing into her upturned face, perusing her features. "With each new day of our acquaintance," he said softly, his attention coming to rest upon her mouth, "I become more convinced that you are the most beautiful woman I have ever known."

Rosalind could not still the mad beating of her heart. Every woman deserved to hear those words at least once in her life, and though she did not doubt Brad's sincerity, she warned herself not to become fanciful once again. "It is the candlelight, sir. Females the world over know how flattering candlelight is to us all."

"Perhaps," he said, "but you have no need of artificial light. Your beauty is illumined by your gentle soul."

With that, he bent and kissed her hand. Softly. Gently. Unhurriedly. The feel of his firm lips warmed her skin; then it seemed to penetrate to her bloodstream, where it traveled upward all along her arm, not stopping until it reached some hitherto undiscovered place within her chest.

When he finally looked up at her, his blue eyes were no longer teasing, and Rosalind fancied they held just a hint of regret. "You are a very special lady," he whispered.

Their gazes held, and with her hand still in his, he straightened and urged her toward him. Unresisting, Rosalind took a step forward. As she waited, her heart pounding painfully against her ribs, Brad lowered his head and touched his lips to hers. It was a gentle kiss, yet while it lasted, waves of warmth swept over her every nerve end, and suddenly everything in her quiet, orderly world went spinning out of control.

During the kiss Rosalind had closed her eyes, hoping to savor the precious moment, but now she opened them. Brad's face was still close to hers, so close she could feel his warm clean breath upon her cheek. She looked at him, at the ruggedly handsome features and the angular line of his jaw, and in that instant she knew she loved him.

Aghast at the revelation, she slipped her hand from his and moved across the room, not stopping until she reached the teak desk. Her knees felt weak, and she had trouble drawing breath into her lungs. Did a person fall in love just like that? At the merest touch of lips upon lips? Or was it possible that she had loved him all along? There had been a feeling there the first time she saw him. At the time she had called it compassion, but had it been something else even then?

Her answer, whatever it might have been, was lost with the moment, as was anything Brad might have wished to say to her in light of the kiss they had shared. Into the silence in the library, the footman intruded, opening the door for Lady Browne.

"So, my boy," her ladyship began upon entering the room, "is it all settled between you? Has the bargain been struck?"

"Yes," Brad replied, his voice oddly husky, "though it may not be the bargain you envisioned."

"What can you mean? Did you or did you not ask Miss Hinton to be your wife?"

"I asked," he said, "and she refused. But I am pleased to inform you that the lady and I have agreed to remain friends."

The dining room was on the same floor as the library, and somehow Rosalind was there, seated at the mahogany table, sipping turtle soup served from an ornate silver tureen. She had no recollection of walking across the corridor, and none of being seated at the table. Those minutes between the present and that moment she had realized she loved Brad seemed to have been absorbed into some sort of celestial vacuum. And no wonder. She had heard that shock did that to people, made them lose track of time.

She sneaked a glance at Brad, who sat opposite her, on his grandmother's right. If he was suffering from a similar shock, he covered it admirably, for he was joking with Lady Browne, teasing her as though he had not a care in the world.

"Really, Brad," the lady admonished, giving his knuckles a rap with her soup spoon, "you are the most incorrigible lad. How can anyone take you seriously when you insist on making light of your experiences? Was the food really so poorly cooked?"

"Worse than poor," he said, rubbing his knuckles. "Unlike this soup, which is excellent. My compliments to the cook. Is it still Mrs. Kershall, by the way?"

"In the prison camp," her ladyship continued, not letting the subject rest, "the food must have been much worse."

When he merely nodded his head, she said, "My boy, were—were you hungry?"

All teasing gone, he reached over and closed his strong fingers around his grandmother's small hand. "Yes," he said, "I was often hungry. But as you see, I did not starve."

Lady Browne closed her eyes, obviously distressed to know that her grandson had suffered privation, and like the lady, Rosalind experienced a sadness that went directly to her heart. *Brad had been hungry.* She had not previously given much thought to such things as supplies, and now she was almost overwhelmed by the realization that the more than ten thousand British soldiers now prisoners of the French were insufficiently fed.

As if reading her thoughts, Brad said, "The French are not so fortunate as the British, who have access to the Portuguese ports and can ship supplies from home to their troops. Though even our own soldiers have much to complain of, for food and ammunition are sometimes unconscionably slow in reaching the men closest to the fighting line. Still, Bonaparte's soldiers fare much worse."

"How so?" Rosalind asked when he paused to enjoy a spoonful of soup.

"Boney's troops are obliged to live off the land," he replied, setting his spoon down and reaching for his wineglass. "That means they must make do with what they can buy or commandeer from the peasant farmers. As you can imagine, the peasants, who have little enough to eat even when they are allowed to keep most of what they grow, do not take kindly to giving the fruits of their labor to the conquering armies. As a result, they despise the French."

"Who can blame them?" Rosalind said.

"No one," Brad replied. "But do not think their hatred of the French means they have any great love for the British soldier, for they do not. As you can imagine, any marching army leaves havoc in its wake, and the poor peasants are constantly caught in the cross fire of the two foreign combatants. No matter which side 'liberates' them, they are still left with burned houses and decimated fields."

This very unsettling information was interrupted by the appearance of the footman who had been sent to Vernon House with Lady Browne's letter. "Ah, Shields," her ladyship said, greeting the liveried servant. "You have returned in good time. I trust my letter was delivered without mishap."

The servant bowed respectfully. "No mishaps, my lady. And it was as you expected, the young lady's relative bid me wait to escort her to town."

"Wonderful. Lady Sizemore is here then?"

"I am," said a plump, middle-aged lady with graying brown hair and blue eyes.

"Aunt!"

Rosalind's back was to the door, but she recognized the voice immediately. Not standing on ceremony, she pushed her chair back and rose from the table, hurrying to the door to throw her arms around Lady Sizemore's shoulders. "Aunt Eudora, you cannot know how glad I am you have come."

"Well, well," the traveler replied, disentangling herself from her niece's embrace, then straightening the lace fichu tucked inside the neck of her stylish purple carriage dress. "You can be no happier to see me than I am to see you, for when I discovered this morning that you had not slept in your bed, I thought you had been kidnapped for certain. La, my dear, I despaired of ever seeing you again."

Lady Sizemore was apparently too excited to notice that everyone was staring at her, for she continued her discourse without a break. 'You can imagine my anxiety, my abject fear, when I was informed that the man who had impersonated poor Lieutenant Ashford was gone as well. Upon hearing of the disappearance of the charlatan—and that is what he is, let Sir Miles say what he will—I got down on my knees and prayed for your safety, my dear girl. For your very life!"

"That was good of you," Rosalind said, the heat of mortification burning her face. "But, I beg of you, Aunt Eudora, say no more upon the subject for the moment. I am persuaded it can wait until we are alone. Instead, allow me to make you known to—"

"It was just too distressing, my love. Only think, the man we all accepted as Sir Miles's nephew was some pretender. And he had the run of the house! We might all have been murdered in our beds. Or worse! Who knows what he might have done if—"

"Aunt! Believe me, this conversation should be postponed until we find ourselves in a more private place. For now, please be so good as to allow me to make you known to your hostess, Lady Browne."

Lady Sizemore blushed, as if only just realizing how rude her behavior must appear. "Forgive me," she said, turning to the smaller lady, who came forward, her hand outstretched in greeting. "You were most kind, Lady Browne, to write explaining my niece's sudden disappearance from Hertfordshire. I was not previously aware that you and she were acquainted, but . . ." She paused, obviously sensing that she was in danger of committing another solipsism. After curtsying, she took the proffered hand. "How do you do? So good of you to invite me."

"Think nothing of it," her hostess said. "It was good of you to join us. Pray allow me to present to you my grandson."

"Of course. Your ladyship is most kind."

"Bradford," his grandmother said, signaling him to come forward, "make your bow to Rosalind's aunt. Lady Sizemore, this is my grandson, Lord Stone."

Eudora Sizemore turned from the well-dressed lady before her, more than happy to make the acquaintance of a titled young gentleman. "Lord Stone," she said, "it is a pleasure to—"

The words caught in her throat, and as she stared at the tall, blond-haired man, her mouth fell open in a most inelegant manner. Pointing an accusing finger, she said, "You! How dare you come here, you . . . you villain!"

Chapter Ten

"But even so, my dear," Lady Sizemore insisted later, when they were alone in Rosalind's bedchamber, "the man kidnapped you." She put her hand upon her ample bosom, as if to still the fluttering within. "My heart fair jumps from my chest at the thought of your being tossed into a carriage and whisked away in the middle of the night."

Rosalind touched the lady's arm to offer what comfort she might. "Do not distress yourself, Aunt Eudora, for as you can see, I came to no harm."

"But I do not see that, my dear. I do not see that at all. Nor, I daresay, will your mother and father when they hear of it. Only think of your reputation. Though Sir Miles was much too worried about the possible safety of his nephew—who I fear is still moldering away in that prison camp—to question your most peculiar absence from his house, I am persuaded your disappearance was the talk of the servants' hall." Though there was no one else in the room, she lowered her voice, as if to avoid being overheard. "You know how servants will gossip."

Rosalind made no reply, for she was only half listening. Aside from the fact that her aunt had been prosing on about the same subject for the past half hour, Rosalind's thoughts were elsewhere.

It had not escaped her notice that when Brad rose from the dining table, he swayed slightly, as though dizzy, and had needed to place his hands upon the back of his chair for just an instant. Nor had she been unaware of his actions after dinner, when they had adjourned to Lady Browne's sitting room. Though he had been subtle about it, Rosalind had seen him use his handkerchief more than once to blot beads of perspiration from his forehead and from his upper lip, and this in a room that was far from warm.

The more she thought about it, the more convinced she became that Brad was still not completely well. He should not have left his sickbed so soon. His wound had been serious, and even if it had been less so, a man who had been undernourished for months was obliged to need more time in which to regain his full health. She appreciated his wish to pass along with all due speed the information he had gathered in the peninsula, but once the task was completed, he should have come home and taken to his bed. Sleep and lots of good, wholesome food were what he needed to recuperate completely.

Rosalind had said nothing to Brad or to his grandmother about what she had seen, for now that his covert mission was completed, she assumed he would take a much-needed rest. It was not until the next morning, when she met him in the small garden at the rear of the town house, that Rosalind was disabused of her erroneous assumption.

Upon coming down to the ground floor, she had looked in first at the dining room where a buffet was laid out for those who wished to break their fast. Brad was not there. Not wanting to reveal how much she wished to see him, she did not ask any of the servants if they knew his whereabouts but strolled out into the garden hoping to meet him by chance. As it transpired, chance was kind to her. Brad stood at the top of the brick walk, his booted foot propped on a wrought iron settee, his attention fixed on something perhaps a million miles from his present location.

It was this fixed stare, coupled with a somber expression upon his face, that first alerted Rosalind to the fact that he had things on his mind—serious things that might not allow him to indulge in the much-needed leisure. With a feeling of foreboding, she approached him, an uneasy smile upon her lips. "Good morning," she said.

When he turned, he fair stole her heart away, for she had never seen him look so handsome. Even though she told herself she saw him through the understandably distorted vision of a woman in love, she doubted that anyone would dispute her appraisal of him. How could they once they beheld him in that slate blue coat? They could not, for the coat was worn over a silver gray waistcoat, and the combination of colors made his eyes appear as though they had been plucked from the clear, mid-May sky.

Those stolen pieces of heaven gazed at her now, and accompanied as they were by a warm, mesmerizing smile, they so unnerved her that she stumbled on one of the bricks of the path.

"Easy there," he said, coming forward and catching her by the shoulders.

The feel of his strong hands further disconcerted her. It was only after they had availed themselves of the wrought iron settee, that Rosalind realized he was telling her that he would be leaving that very afternoon for Portsmouth. "My ultimate destination is the Iberian Peninsula," he said.

Rosalind was unable to believe her ears. "You are returning to Portugal?"

In answer to her question, he said, "The schedule I investigated yesterday was for ships leaving Portsmouth, bound for Oporto. When I discovered that one such vessel sets sail in two days' time, I arranged passage aboard her. With any luck, I should be on the peninsula in little more than a fortnight."

He spoke calmly enough, as though returning to a war-torn country was as harmless a journey as riding through Hyde Park, yet all the while Rosalind listened to his plans, fear for him caused her lungs to constrict painfully in her chest. "I cannot believe they gave you another assignment."

"They? The War Office, do you mean? They did not."

She caught hold of his sleeve. "Then why must you go? I—I have been watching you. You are not well enough to undertake such a journey."

"How well does a man have to be before he does the right thing?"

The question being unanswerable, Rosalind merely looked at him. "I do not understand."

"George Ashford is still imprisoned," he said quietly.

"But what has that to do with—"

"I must go back for him. Surely you must see that. The repatriation was meant for Ashford, not for me."

When she stared at him, her mouth agape, Brad said, "I cannot in good conscience allow Ashford to remain there. You do not know what it is like in the camp."

He was correct. Rosalind did not know; however, she recalled with frightening clarity what Brad had disclosed to his grandmother just the night before. *"I was often hungry,"* he had said. At that time the words had tugged at Rosalind's heart; now, of course, they grabbed that vital organ and squeezed it without mercy.

"The lieutenant wanted you to get the medical attention you needed," she said. "He was grateful to you for saving his life, as any gentleman would have been. Sending you home in his stead was the honorable thing to do. A man like Ashford could have done no less."

Brad laid his hand over hers where it still rested on his sleeve. "And would you have me be less honorable than the lieutenant?"

Yes! Yes! If it will keep you safe.

Rosalind wanted to say the words—scream them if that was what was needed to make him listen—but they would not come. Deep inside her, she knew there were no words potent enough to convince him to remain in England where he was out of harm's way, warm and well fed. Not while the man responsible for his safe return languished in a French prison camp.

She knew enough of Brad Stone to know that honor was as much a part of him as his blond hair and his blue eyes. If it were not so, she would not love him as fiercely as she did. Resigned to the fact that no argument would disuade him from his chosen course, she asked quietly, "Will you drive or go by post?"

"Neither. My grandmother has expressed a desire to go down with me, to see me off. We will take her traveling coach."

"Lady Browne accompanies you to Portsmouth?"

"Just for the night," he replied. "Then she goes on to Stoneleigh Park where she will await my return. I believe I told you my home is in Sussex. The park is near Bilchester, which is little more than an hour's drive from Portsmouth."

Rosalind was about to wish him "Godspeed" when an idea occurred to her. The idea was rash, and so unlike the Rosalind Hinton of one week ago that she vowed to set her plan in motion immediately, before she lost her nerve. Matching action to the thought, she rose from the wrought iron settee. "If you will excuse me," she said, "I must go inside now."

"By all means," he replied, standing as well. "Have you broken your fast? If not, will you join me? I find I am more than ready to—"

"No, I thank you," she said, "but I am not hungry."

Before he could detain her further, Rosalind hurried along the brick path toward the French windows. During the few minutes needed to reach the house, then rush through the library and up the stairs to Lady Browne's bedchamber, Rosalind rehearsed the request she meant to put to Brad's grandmother. What she would do if the lady refused her, she did not know, but one way or another, she was going to Portsmouth.

"Of course you may accompany us," her ladyship said, a look of satisfaction on her face. "Did I not say you were like me? If it had been my Harold leaving for foreign lands, I would not have let him go without a proper goodbye."

The lady sighed. "There is a certain kind of woman who gives her heart but once, and when she loves, she does so with all her soul. I was one of those women, and I believe, my child, that you are the same.''

Rosalind considered denying the allegation. On second thought, she decided to save her breath, for if she was able to bring her entire plan to fruition, there would be no hiding her feelings from the world.

As if reading her thoughts, Lady Browne said, "If it had been my Harold going to Portugal, I would have found a way to go with him. But then, you modern young ladies are so circumspect, not nearly as impetuous as I was.''

Lady Browne may have deemed the modern young ladies lacking in impetuosity, but Rosalind's aunt took an entirely different view of the matter. ''Have you taken complete leave of your senses!''

Lady Sizemore's question being unanswerable, it hung in the air between them. Finally, Rosalind said, ''If you should dislike the idea of traveling south, Aunt Eudora, you have only to remain here until I return. Or you may return to Oxfordshire.''

''Return home! Without you. My dear girl, how would I ever explain your absence to your parents?''

''You may tell them the truth.''

''And have my sister-in-law ring a peal over me for not being a proper chaperon? I thank you, no.''

''As you wish, Aunt. Whatever your decision, I am determined to accompany Lady Browne as far as Portsmouth.''

Somewhat taken aback by her niece's resolve, the lady said, ''But what is your purpose?''

''Must there be one?''

''Certainly there must. I could appreciate your desire to wish Lord Stone a *bon voyage* if you cherished some sort of particularity of regard for him. Obviously that is

not the situation, for if it were, you would not have seen
fit to refuse his very flattering offer for your hand. And
since there is not even the chance of an understanding
between the two of you, I cannot perceive of any necessity for your seeing him off.''

''Nonetheless, ma'am, I am determined upon the
action.''

As it transpired, Rosalind and both their ladyships
made the ninety mile trip to the noisy, energetic port
city, with Brad riding on a spirited gray gelding for most
of the journey, and only occasionally joining them in
the well-appointed traveling coach. On one of those
respites, when Rosalind studied his face in the shadowed
enclosure, she fancied he looked rather tired. Of course,
she kept her opinions to herself, for she knew all too
well that he would not appreciate any solicitousness on
her part. Unfortunately, she could not stop her
thoughts, and they plagued her with visions of Brad
alone and friendless in a war-torn country, with no one
to offer him aid should he become ill.

All that afternoon and the next day, as they continued
on their way to Portsmouth, those unsettling pictures
vexed her. Though she tried to appear calm during
their farewell dinner at the picturesque Old Ship Inn,
the audacity of what she planned to do made her far
too nervous to contribute anything of interest to the
conversation. Unfortunately, the private rooms at the
Old Ship were small, and with the four diners sitting
quite close around the candlelit table, it was difficult to
hide the fact that one of the quartet had other things
on her mind.

"You are unusually quiet this evening, my friend," Brad said.

Not wanting him, or their ladyships, to suspect what she contemplated doing, Rosalind replied, "Forgive my lack of conversation, sir. I fear my thoughts were elsewhere."

"Can you not share them with us?" he asked.

When she shook her head, he said, "An ill omen, indeed."

He turned to his grandmother then, a teasing tone in his voice. "I regret to inform you, ma'am, that the last time I saw Rosalind this quiet, the evening ended with me staring down the barrel of a dueling pistol."

While Lady Browne *tsk tisked*, he returned his attention to Rosalind. "May I hope a repeat of that incident is not in my future?"

Rosalind chuckled, finding it impossible not to respond to his teasing. "You are a cad, sir, to persist in airing my past mistakes. Naturally, you force me to retaliate by reminding you that *your* actions that evening were not wholly admirable."

He waved aside her remark. "Surely you cannot mean to compare the two acts?"

"Certainly not, for there can be no comparison. One act was merely ill advised, the other was illegal."

"I quite agree, madam. *You* pursued me with a potentially lethal weapon, while *I* did no more than give you a boost into a departing carriage."

"Against my will!"

When he feigned indifference to her accusation, Rosalind said, "It may interest you to know, sir, that for the sort of assistance you supplied, it is the custom to reward the 'booster' with transportation to the penal colony in Australia."

Rosalind bit her lip at the thoughtless remark, for a penal colony was too reminiscent of the French prison camp. If Brad connected the two, however, he showed no sign of it. On the contrary, his lips twitched at the corners as though he tried to suppress a smile. "I concede the point, madam, my crime was the most heinous, and never again will I enter into debate with you."

Rosalind knew he spoke in jest, but the words, "never again," settled upon her heart like some momentous premonition. Afraid he might see the distress in her eyes, she busied herself with arranging her fork and knife upon her plate to indicate that she had eaten all she wished of her meal.

She said nothing more until the waiter had finished removing what remained of the platter of buttered prawns and the bowl of fricassee of turnips, replacing them with an apricot trifle redolent of just-ignited brandy. As the blue and orange flames fired up, then were quickly extinguished, Rosalind placed her napkin upon the table and asked if she might be forgiven for refusing the sweet in favor of an early night. "I fear the journey has left me rather tired, and I should like nothing better than to retire to my bed."

"My dear," Lady Sizemore said, "are you sickening from something? Shall I come up with you, or perhaps procure a tisane?"

"No!"

Realizing that her aunt's mouth was agape with astonishment, Rosalind replied more calmly, "I thank you, Aunt Eudora, but I shall be right as a trivet once I have had a night's rest." Then, very casually, she added, "I daresay I shall be asleep the instant my head touches the pillow, so I beg you will not stop by my room when you retire."

"As you wish," the affronted lady replied. "I should not dream of disturbing you."

Into the silence that followed this small contretemps, Brad said, "Allow me to see you to your room."

He rose from the table and walked around to hold Rosalind's chair, and she, grateful for the distraction, bid her aunt and Lady Browne a hasty good evening and allowed Brad to escort her from the private parlor. At the foot of the stairs, she paused. "Good night, sir."

"I shall see you safely up to your chamber," he said.

She shook her head. "I should prefer that you did not."

His eyebrows lifted in surprise at her refusal, but when she held out her hand, he took it, obliged to accept her decision. "Rosalind, if I have done anything to offend you, please—"

"You have done nothing, sir. As I said earlier, I am merely tired and in need of my bed. And should I oversleep and not come down before you leave tomorrow, allow me to wish you a safe journey."

His eyes darkened for an instant, but the look was gone before Rosalind could determine its significance. It might have been regret, but it might just as easily have been a reflection of the candle stub that guttered in the wall sconce.

He lifted her hand to his lips. "I shall miss you, my friend."

Tears stung Rosalind's eyes, and afraid she would give herself away if she did not leave immediately, she pulled her hand from his and hurried up the stairs. She did not look back; she did not even pause until she was safely inside her bedchamber with the door locked securely behind her.

"At last," she said, her breath ragged, as though she

had run up a dozen flights of stairs rather than only one. "I thought I would never get away."

"*Oui, mademoiselle.* But you are here now, and you must hurry, *s'il vous plâit.*"

Rosalind looked toward the bed, where clothing had been laid out in readiness for her. "What of the hackney?"

"The coachman, he is in the taproom as we speak, but he will be in the stable yard in fifteen minutes. I promised him double his fare, so have no fear, he will wait for you."

"Excellent. Thank you, Clotilde. Now, what do we do first?"

"First, *mademoiselle*, we bind up the bosoms."

Twenty minutes later, holding a single candle aloft, Lady Browne's middle-aged maid ushered a young lad down the servants stairs to the kitchen entrance of the Old Ship Inn. The youth—fourteen or fifteen years old, judging by his height and slight build—was dressed in faded, slightly ragged nankeen breeches, over which he wore an ill-fitting frieze jacket. A spotted blue bandanna handkerchief had been tied loosely around his neck so that it extended somewhat over his chin, and pulled down low on his head was a billed cap whose dark drugget was noticeably threadbare.

Neither maid nor lad spoke until they were outside in the stable yard. "*Voila,*" Clotilde whispered. "There is the hackney, complete with driver."

The lad looked where the maid pointed, then breathed a sigh of relief. "Thank you, Clotilde. I could not have done this without your help. The clothes, the carriage, I cannot begin to tell you how much I appreciate—"

"Yes, yes," the maid whispered. "But you must go now, *mademoiselle,* for time, she is running out."

Pausing only long enough to hug the woman's thin shoulders, Rosalind hurried across the stable yard and climbed inside the public carriage. As soon as the door was closed, the jarvey, having been informed earlier of the lad's destination, gave the rawboned old horse the signal. Within less than a minute the metallic *clop, clop* of the shod hooves could be heard on the cobblestone street outside the inn.

While the hackney made its way through the always busy streets of Portsmouth, heading toward the even busier docks, the maid slipped unobtrusively into the private parlor where her mistress was enjoying an after-dinner cup of tea in the company of her grandson and Lady Sizemore. Catching Lady Browne's eye, Clotilde nodded briefly, whereupon her ladyship sighed then settled more comfortably in her chair, a smile of satisfaction upon her lips.

The square-rigged sails of *The Stormy Petrel* were filled with air, and as the light, trim frigate sped southward, it bounded over the waves. In its wake it left behind the breathtaking, near-vertical chalk sea cliffs to its right and the mist-shrouded channel islands to its left. While the ship forsook the rolling swells of the Channel for the even-rougher waters of the North Atlantic, Brad stood at the polished wood rails, enjoying the blue-gray of the morning sky.

Knowing better than to trust his hat to the vicissitudes of the wind, he held the broad-brimmed felt in his hands, enjoying the feel of the fresh breeze blowing through his hair. He breathed deeply, filling his lungs with the clean, briny air, then he licked his lips, tasting the salty sea spray that was already forming a thin crystalline layer upon his skin.

The parting at the Old Ship Inn early that morning had not been easy, for his grandmother had been obliged to hide the tears that glistened in her eyes, and Rosalind had not come down at all to bid him farewell. Even so, it was wonderful to be underway at last, for the sooner he got to Oporto and made arrangements for the trip to the Spanish border, the sooner he could purchase Lieutenant George Ashford's release from the French prisoner-of-war camp. Once Ashford was safe, and returned to his home in Hertfordshire, Brad would be free of the burden of guilt he carried on the soldier's behalf.

"Have you found your sea legs yet, sir?"

"I have," Brad replied, turning to look at the leathery-faced old captain. Angus Newsome had cupped his hands on either side of his mouth so his words would not be swept away by the wind, and Brad did the same.

"An hour or two is usually all I need, Captain. I am fast becoming a seasoned sailor."

"Happy to hear it, sir."

The captain touched his finger to his forehead in quasi salute, then he turned to continue toward the bridge. He had taken only a few steps when he stopped. "Lord Stone," he said, "I did not ask after your servant. The swells are unusually high for this time of year. Is the lad experiencing any sea sickness?"

"Servant?" Thinking the captain had him confused with one of the other passengers, Brad said, "I am traveling alo—"

"The youngster seemed quite nervous when he came aboard and asked for your cabin. I thought perhaps this was his first time putting out to sea, and if that is true, he may find the crossing difficult. Oh, well, if this wind holds, the trip will be short, and we should be in Oporto in about ten days. I daresay the boy will not expire in the meantime."

With that the captain was gone, leaving Brad to wonder why anyone—lad or no—should be asking for his cabin. Determined to know the answer, he abandoned his position at the rail and went below, his objective to discover for himself the identity of the possible stowaway.

Brad paused before the door of his cabin, listening for a full minute. When he heard nothing, he released the latch and eased the door open. The cabin, though first class, was unbelievably small, outfitted with a single chair, a two-drawer washstand upon which reposed an encased washbowl and pitcher, and a narrow cot which was suspended by chains from the ceiling.

Upon the swaying cot, his back to the door, lay a slender youth dressed in ragged nankeen breeches and a frieze jacket. Apparently he did not suffer from the vexations of sea sickness, and if the sound of his soft, even breathing was any indication, the motion of the ship had rocked him to sleep. It was nothing to Brad if the lad stowed away—the righting of that wrong he would leave to the captain of the vessel—but he very much disliked the idea of this unknown boy using *his* name to worm his way on board.

Not bothering to close the door behind him, Brad stepped inside the cabin and reached for the stowaway. After grabbing him by the collar of his ill-fitting jacket, he gave one quick yank that tumbled the lad from the cot onto the hardwood floor. With arms and legs flying, the slight body fell ignominiously, and the soft thud of his landing was followed by a rather high-pitched squeal of protest.

To Brad's surprise, as the urchin scrambled to gain his feet, his dark billed cap fell off, releasing a mass of rich brown curls that spilled all about his back and shoulders. At the sight of all that hair, Brad groaned, for he knew only one person in the world who possessed tresses that thick and lustrous.

But what in the name of all that was holy was she doing aboard *The Stormy Petrel*?

Chapter Eleven

"Damnation, woman! Why are you not back at the Old Ship Inn? What in hell possessed you to stow away aboard this vessel?"

While Brad kicked the cabin door shut, Rosalind scurried to her feet. Unfortunately, she had no place to go, so she stood perfectly still, the sharp corner of the washstand poking a hole in her back. Hoping to regain a bit of her dignity, she said, "I told you the other evening that I do not like to be railed at."

"A pity, madam, for this time you will endure whatever I choose to say. If I am denied verbal release, I might be obliged to resort to violence, and believe me, at this moment, wringing your lovely neck ranks very high on the list of things I would like to do. Now, before I lose my temper completely, I want an answer. Why are you here?"

Rosalind had never seen Brad so angry. Though she could well understand his annoyance, she questioned the advisability of telling him at just that moment that she had come to help keep him safe. "Your purpose in coming to Portugal is to free Lieutenant Ashford. My purpose in coming is to accompany you to the Spanish border. When you free the lieutenant, I will be there to help."

"Are you mad! You cannot travel with me all the way to the border."

"Why can I not?"

"For one thing, it would be unseemly. For another, it would be beyond your physical endurance."

He could not have offered arguments more suited to encourage her continued effort. As for those final two words, it was *his* physical endurance that concerned her. His well-being was her primary reason for being there. He needed someone to protect his back, and she meant to be that one. "I am stronger than I look."

"No," he said, the word emphatic, "you are not."

Hoping to draw a smile from him, she made a fist, then she bent her arm, exhibiting her bicep. "Feel that," she said, indicating the minuscule bulge beneath the sleeve of her jacket.

Her attempt to amuse him failed miserably. She had never seen him look less like smiling, even after he cast a cursory glance at her sleeve. There was, however, a rather calculating look in his eyes.

"That is the best you can do for a muscle?" he asked.

Before Rosalind suspected what he was about, Brad reached out with his right hand and grabbed her shoulder, just below her neck. In the next instant she was being spun around and pulled hard against his chest, and his forearm was across her throat, cutting off her air supply.

Shocked beyond belief at such treatment, and unable

to draw breath, she clutched at his rocklike arm, trying with all her might to pull it away from her throat. Her efforts were futile. He was much too strong for her, and though she clawed the skin of his hand and wrist, drawing blood, he did not let her go.

Finally, when she thought she would faint from the lack of air, he relaxed his hold on her, then he leaned down and whispered into her ear. "That, my dear, is a muscle."

Not yet finished with her, he said, "Between here and the Spanish border there are at least a hundred thousand soldiers, and a surprising number of them are every bit as strong as me. Some are even stronger."

Still holding her prisoner, he reached around her with his free arm and caught a fistful of her hair, bringing it back across her face like a veil. "There is something else you may not know about those hundred thousand soldiers."

"What?" she asked, the word little better than a whisper.

"There is not a man jack of them who does not spend his nights dreaming of getting his hands on hair such as this."

He let go her hair and put his arm around her waist, encircling it almost painfully tight. "I will not sully your ears with what those men dream of doing to such a figure."

His actions had spoken more powerfully than his words, and it required all Rosalind's bravado to speak. "You do not disuade me," she said.

"Then you are more fool than I would had thought possible."

With that, he let her go, stepping back as far as the

small space would allow. "You would risk your safety for Lieutenant Ashford?"

When Rosalind declined to answer his question, the anger left Brad's face, replaced by a bewildered look. In a matter of seconds, something else supplanted the bewilderment. "Madam, I had not previously suspected that Ashford's welfare was so important to you."

"Sir, you have no idea what—or who—is important to me."

They argued for the better part of the day, with Brad finally storming out for a walk around the deck, instructing her in no uncertain terms that she was not to leave the cabin. He had no idea what he was to do with her. If only *The Stormy Petrel* were returning to England, he could pay Rosalind's passage and trust Captain Newsome to see her safely delivered to Portsmouth. Unfortunately, once the frigate left Oporto, it was scheduled to continue to Lisbon, and from there its destination was the Gold Coast in Africa.

Brad had no recourse but to take Rosalind ashore with him, and once they were on land, he would search out some respectable female to take her in until his return. Not that he expected the task to be easy. There was no knowing what may have transpired in the village in the last few days.

While at the War Office four days ago, Brad had heard that the French had overrun Oporto after the battle of Corunna. Fortunately, the British forces, under the leadership of General Arthur Wellesley, had retaken the village as recently as two weeks ago. Still, with the battle so recent, there might be no decent females in residence. Even if there were, they might not wish to take into their homes a young lady so lost to propriety as to don the clothes of a street urchin and stow away on a frigate.

Nor would the pseudo street urchin like the idea of being left behind. Anticipating her reaction, and wanting to delay for as long as possible the inescapable argument, Brad decided not to return to the cabin until after *The Stormy Petrel* had reached the lovely old village of Oporto.

What the captain and crew thought of a man who purchased a second cabin, giving over the original to his servant, Brad did not ask. Trading on his dignity as Lord Stone, he merely requested that the lad be served his meals in the cabin and that any books aboard ship might be put at the boy's disposal.

He did not approach the cabin again until nine days later, when the frigate reached Portugal.

Standing at the rail as they approached land, he closed his ears to the shouting of orders and the sound of sailors running back and forth on deck, busy with the tasks of bringing the ship to a safe docking. Instead he watched for his first sight of the vine-laden hillsides and the old red-roofed houses.

As always the *Torre dos Clerigo* was first to appear, for the eighteenth century granite Tower of the Clerics reached more than two hundred feet into the air and could be seen clearly at a distance, even in the gathering dusk. As the ship drew closer to shore, Brad spied the twelfth century cathedral as well, and finally the hundreds of ancient little dwellings that appeared to be stacked one atop the other, wedged into the steep slopes of the mountainside.

When the frigate was securely docked, and the warm, humid air of Portugal began to envelope it, Brad went below for Rosalind. She answered his knock promptly, greeting him with a serene countenance, which was a rather surprising circumstance considering her solitary confinement. Though he had expected some justified resentment on her part, Brad was grateful for the calm, especially since they were obliged to make their way through several dozen deckhands without giving any of them cause to suspect that the serving lad was, in fact, a female in disguise.

Brad bid her walk behind him, carrying his small valise like a proper servant, and to say nothing while they disembarked the ship. With this Rosalind complied meekly enough. It was only later, after they were ashore and traversing the narrow cobbled streets, that her assertiveness resurfaced. It was then he informed her of his plans to leave her there in the village.

"Do not waste your time searching out that respectable female," she told him quietly, "for I will not stay with her. Under no circumstances will I remain behind."

"And under no circumstances will I allow you to accompany me," he countered sharply. Her calm refusal irritated him almost more than the outburst he had expected.

"Then we are at an impasse."

"No, madam, we are not, for you will do as I say and remain here in Oporto. Portugal is a wild country, and in the north, which is the route I must take, the terrain is quite mountainous. Travel is difficult at the best of times, and with Bonaparte's soldiers scattered throughout the peninsula, I can assure you, these are the worst of times."

She listened politely to his words, but when he was finished, she said, "If you will not take me with you, you leave me no option but to follow you on my own."

"Are you insane!"

"No. Determined."

They were headed down a dreary, narrow little street toward an old tavern where Brad had stayed when he was in the village more than a year ago, but when he heard the determination in Rosalind's voice he stopped. Catching her by the elbow, he turned her so he could look into her face. What he saw dealt him a felling blow, for he had never seen a more resolute countenance.

Heaven help him! She meant what she said. Hers was no idle threat. She would follow him across this wild, dangerous country.

And all to save George Ashford!

After mentally cataloging the various dangers inherent in a trip to the Spanish border—dangers that multiplied if the traveler was a beautiful woman—Brad was forced to admit that Rosalind would be safer in his company than trailing behind him. Unable to deny the truth, he surrendered.

As quick as the snap of a finger, the decision was made. Like that, it was a *fait accompli*. "Turn around," he said finally, the order brusque, "and let me have a look at you."

A smile lit her face, and it seemed to Brad that the sun had come out, warming him and brightening the dim, shabby little street. "Of course," she replied. "Whatever you say." As though to show her willingness to cooperate now that he had capitulated, Rosalind pirouetted for him, letting him observe her from every angle.

Still reeling from the surprise of discovering how much pleasure it gave him to give her what she wanted, Brad tried in vain to ignore that beautiful smile and the strange effect it had upon the thrumming of his pulse.

While he watched her twirl happily before him, he experienced even more difficulty purging from his thoughts the sudden rather fierce desire to gather her in his arms and smother her with kisses—kisses meant to make her forgot all about Lieutenant George Ashford.

To give his thoughts a new direction, Brad concentrated his attention upon her costume, looking her over from the coarse wool cap down to the cheap boots. The breeches and jacket were loose-fitting and bulky enough to conceal her quite feminine curves, and if no one examined her too closely she might, indeed, pass for a lad. That is, if she managed to keep her hair hidden securely beneath the cap.

Recalling how the beautiful tresses had spilled about her shoulders when he had snatched her out of the cot in the cabin, he said, "Your hair might give you away. You will want to do something about it before we begin the journey. Can you braid it, perhaps?"

This time her smile was impish. "There is no need. I took care of it several days ago, while you were ignoring me."

Before he could ask what she meant, she whisked off the cap. He expected the gorgeous tresses to come tumbling down, and when they did not, he blinked his eyelids, hoping that what he saw was some sort of mirage brought about by the warm, humid Portuguese air. It was no illusion. Her locks were raggedly shorn, like those of some loutish plowboy, with the thick strands now barely two inches long.

Slowly Brad reached out and touched her head, allowing the too-short hair to brush against his palm. Still staring at her, he caught one of the raggedly cut locks and rubbed it between his fingertips, as if he needed to employ some other sense to confirm the travesty his eyes refused to believe.

"Damnation," he muttered. It was the best he could do under the circumstances, for he felt betrayed. He felt as though she had stolen something from him—something he had not yet had an opportunity to experience, something he had not yet had an opportunity to enjoy. Yet how could he tell her that. He could not. Instead he said, "Rosalind, what in heaven's name have you done?"

Brad had warned her that the tavern was far from elegant, but when they reached it, Rosalind found it was even more disreputable than he had predicted. Since he had seen the place last, bullet holes had scarred the ancient wooden doors, giving evidence of Oporto's occupation by a conquering army. Gauge marks now showed all around the windows, where someone had used a sword to dislodge the beautiful decorative tiles that were so much a part of the culture of the country.

When she and Brad entered the small, dimly lit establishment, Rosalind tried not to notice the rough-looking men who sat around the wobbly wooden tables, talking quietly and drinking port wine, the aromatic distilled wine made in the nearby hills and named for the village. The men seemed a wary-eyed, suspicious lot, and the tension in the room was thick enough to stop a raging bull.

Brad had warned her to remain silent—a quite superfluous instruction, for after nine days of solitude she was growing accustomed to silence—but she could not have spoken if her life had depended upon it. She was so nervous her mouth had dried up completely, making speech impossible. Brad had no such difficulty, however, and he bid a good evening to the distrustful-looking man who stood behind the once-handsome mahogany counter. *"Dao noite, Senhor."*

Rosalind stared at Brad in surprise, for his Portuguese was every bit as fluent and accentless as his French.

Hearing his own language, the man's manner relaxed. *"Dao noite,"* he replied.

"Do you remember me?" Brad asked.

"I do, *Senhor*. How may I help you?"

The two men spoke quietly, then several silver coins were passed across the counter, only to be snatched up quickly by the aproned proprietor. Two minutes later Rosalind and Brad were abovestairs, standing in the center of a small, dark chamber situated over the taproom. The room's one small window was crusted with grime, and in place of a candle, a single strip of cloth submerged in meat fat supplied the only light.

"I must go out," Brad told her almost the moment they arrived. "I have arrangements to make and some purchases." He looked at her, a warning in his eyes. "Can I trust you to wait for me here?"

When she nodded, he said, "Good. Get some rest if you can, for we will leave at first light in the morning."

"But what of you? You need rest as well."

"Tomorrow," he said.

Since he quit the room without another word, closing the door softly behind him and locking it with the big iron key, Rosalind was obliged to make what she would of his reply. Realizing that she could do nothing until he returned, she removed her cap and boots and laid down on the small, straw-filled mattress that occupied most of the floor. She tried not to notice the combined aromas of male sweat and wet dog that permeated the

ticking, for if what Brad told her was true, before the
week was out, she would probably consider this luxury.

The next morning she awoke surprisingly refreshed,
and after eating the crusty brown bread and the rich
soft cheese she assumed Brad had set just inside the
door, Rosalind washed her face, donned her cap and
boots, and went belowstairs. Brad was nowhere in sight;
the tavern was empty save for two men. Both men were
dressed in the rough twill trousers and weskits of the
laborer, and neither of them had removed his droopy,
sweat-stained hat. They sat at separate tables, each
silently sipping strong, aromatic coffee, and though they
seemed to ignore her, she felt their eyes boring into
her back when she walked to the open door and looked
outside.

Where was Brad?

Following his instructions not to so much as open
her mouth, she stepped outside the tavern and sat down
on the sun-warmed cobbles. She pulled her knees up
to her chest as she had seen many a young boy do; then
she crossed her arms over her knees and rested her
chin upon her forearm. Not knowing what else to do,
she stared off into space and prayed that Brad would
appear before someone became suspicious and questioned her for loitering on the street.

She had been there no more than a minute when
she heard the scrape of a chair across the stone floor.
Turning back to look inside the tavern, she watched
one of the laborers, a tall, broad-shouldered fellow, set
his empty cup on the table, toss a copper coin beside
it, then stand and sling an old cloth satchel over his
shoulder.

As he stepped past her, the man tapped the side of her foot with the toe of his boot. *"Venha comigo,"* he muttered. At the sound of the deep voice, Rosalind looked up, happier than she had thought possible to recognize the clear blue eyes that were all but obscured by the drooping hat brim.

Assuming he had told her to come with him, she scurried up from the cobbles. Brad had not waited for her, but was halfway down the street, his long legs carrying him at a quick pace. Obliged to run to catch up with him, Rosalind was sorely tempted to give him a piece of her mind for making her think he had left her. But when she was beside him, looking up into his face, she saw that this had been a test.

Thankfully she had passed.

Brad said nothing, but the look of approval in his eyes sent a glow of warmth through Rosalind's entire body—a glow more to be desired than all the medals in the kingdom. Vowing to keep her tongue between her teeth forever if it would earn her more such unspoken praise, she hurried along, very nearly keeping step with Brad's athletic gait.

They walked for about a mile, until they came to a broad, deep river that apparently flowed from the east to empty its clear waters into the nearby Atlantic. Standing on the south bank, Rosalind could see across the wide expanse to the north bank, which boasted two sturdy wharves erected in front of a series of steep hills. The principle feature of those hills was several dozen large caves.

Eight or ten long, shallow-keel sailboats were tied up at the wharves, and men in sailor's garb of twill trousers, secured at the waist by intricately knotted cord, unloaded the cargo of large, wooden barrels. The barrels were rolled up planks leading to the caves, and as they rolled, they made a deep, rumbling sound that drifted across the river.

For the benefit of anyone who might be watching them, Brad gave Rosalind's shoulder a playful punch. Then in the manner of an actor in a play, he laughed and said something to her in rapid Portuguese. She smiled and nodded. Though she found most of what he had said unintelligible, she had caught one phrase, something that sounded like port wine. Assuming he meant to inform her that the barrels being stored in the caves were filled with wine, she nodded again and said, "*Sim, senhor.*"

Momentarily startled by her reply, even if it was only a simple, "Yes, sir," Brad covered his surprise with another hearty laugh. He gave her another Portuguese earful that ended with his pointing to the sailboats and calling them something that sounded like *barcos rabelo*. This time she merely nodded.

Last evening, before he left her, Brad had said the first half of their journey eastward would be traveled on the *Douro Rio*, their mode of transportation the sailboats that transported the wine from Regua, in the interior. One such boat had unloaded its last keg and was even then crossing the wide river, headed in their direction, its auxiliary oars slapping the peaceful water. Within a matter of minutes, the two crewmen had pulled in their oars and the boat was drifting toward the wharf.

"*Bom dia, senhor,*" the captain called in greeting as he tossed the line to Brad.

"*Bom dia,*" Brad replied politely, catching the line and draping it over a piling.

The captain, a tall, mahogany-skinned fellow with straight black hair and a bushy mustache that must have measured eight inches on either side of his mouth, jumped onto the wharf. Immediately he and Brad entered into a hushed argument that involved a great deal of posturing and head shaking.

"*Não,*" the man said emphatically, pretending to turn and reboard the boat. "*Não. Não.*"

Brad had warned her about the Iberians' penchant for haggling, so she was not as astonished as she might have been by the man's negative response.

The captain did not board the boat, of course, and when he returned, the bargaining resumed, lasting for perhaps five minutes. At the end of the negotiations, Brad and the captain shook hands, both apparently satisfied with the deal struck. During the handshake, a small pouch of coins was passed to the mustached gentleman, who slapped Brad on the back in cheerful camaraderie then waved him on board.

The *barco rabelo* was an exciting mode of transportation, for once the big square mainsail was hoisted, it filled with the breeze that was a constant feature of the Douro valley. They seemed to glide along at an unlooked-for speed. As they traveled eastward, Rosalind spied workers on either side of the river, gathering the grapes from tiered vineyards that rose almost to the heavens.

In the distance, behind the vineyards, green broad-crowned trees beckoned invitingly. Faced with such an idyllic scene, Rosalind was obliged to remind herself that things were seldom as uncomplicated as they appeared, and that this lovely country and her people were under constant threat by one military force or another.

The trip lasted fully seven hours, and though Rosalind found another stint of forced silence a bit trying, Brad had no such problem. Directly after they came aboard, he found a shaded corner where the kegs were generally stowed and made himself comfortable, placing the cloth satchel containing their belongings behind his back and stretching his long legs out in front of him. In a surprisingly short time he was asleep, his soft breathing blending with the soothing sound of water splashing against the bow of the boat.

Now, of course, Rosalind understood what Brad had meant last night when he said he would rest tomorrow. Happy to see him get some much-needed sleep, she contented herself with watching the passing scenery. For a time it was all lush vineyards, but as they continued eastward through the valley, the terrain became less verdant, less hospitable. On either side of the Douro, the riverbanks became rocky, while the mountains in the distance appeared higher, more formidable.

The captain and his crewmen went about their jobs, someone always at the tiller, and someone constantly trimming the sails to take full advantage of the available wind. None of the three bothered to enlist Rosalind in conversation; she assumed her disguise had convinced them that she was a young boy.

Once during the trip, one of the sailors had approached her, offering her an earthenware bowl filled to the rim with freshly cooked fish chowder. Rosalind had not understood his words, but her nose recognized a universal language. When her mouth began to water at the tempting aroma of spices, vegetables, and thick chunks of sardine, she accepted the bowl and nodded her thanks.

She ate every last morsel of the delicious concoction, and if she had known how to do so, she would have asked for more. Instead, she merely returned the bowl to the crewman. *"Obrigado,"* she said, hoping the word meant, "Thank you."

When the man nodded, she smiled, pleased to know she had spoken correctly.

Some time later, Brad opened his eyes. Because Rosalind sat not more than an arm's length away from him, she was in his line of vision, and when he saw her, he smiled sleepily. The smile was warm and sincere, and it caused a sudden acceleration in the rhythm of her breathing.

Though she tried to ignore the quickened breaths, they accelerated even more when Brad stretched languidly, flexing the muscles in his arms and unintentionally causing all manner of fascinating ripples across his broad back. It was all Rosalind could do not to reach over and touch him, for she longed to feel those masculine ripples beneath her fingers.

She called herself a wanton for even contemplating such action, and because she was afraid Brad would read her thoughts, she tried to focus on something other than the man beside her. Inadvertently, he furnished a most effective diversion, for when he turned to retrieve the satchel he had used for a pillow, his weskit fell open, and she saw a sheathed knife hanging against his left ribs. It was a slender weapon, but the blade was long and so lethal-looking that the very sight of it caused Rosalind to gasp.

To cover the noise of her reaction, she feigned a bout of coughing; then she turned away, busying herself with looking about for the cap she had removed earlier to allow the breeze to blow through her short hair. It was strange, but just knowing that Brad carried such a menacing weapon—something silent and hidden, like a poisonous viper coiled and ready to strike—brought home to her the dangers they might soon face.

He had warned her about the perils, and she had thought she understood. She had not. The instant she saw the knife, she realized she had entered a world she knew nothing about—one in which survival depended upon one's ability to defend oneself. In this world, the man she loved might be called upon to use a deadly weapon against men who wore weapons of their own— men who would think nothing of taking his life. Or hers.

At the thought, a shiver ran through her. Though Rosalind would not wish herself any place but alongside Brad, she offered up a prayer to heaven that her being with him would not put his life at further risk. While she made her silent plea, Brad came to his feet and reached down for the satchel, slinging it over his shoulder. *"Sehor,"* he called to the captain.

"Venha," the captain replied, motioning Brad aft, where he sat manning the long wooden tiller.

While the two men conversed, Brad was given a bowl of the fish chowder. He ate the food quickly, without seeming to notice the delicious flavor; he was far too intent on whatever he and the captain were discussing. The gist of their conversation was lost on Rosalind, but when they rounded the next meander of the *Douro Rio,* the captain yelled something to the crewmen, who promptly hauled in the sail and positioned the oars. In a matter of minutes they had rowed the boat to within two or three feet of the rocky riverbank.

"Obrigado," Brad called out to the captain.

"Não tem de quê," the man replied, touching his finger to the bill of his cap.

Rosalind was still looking at the captain when Brad

grabbed her by the wrist and, without so much as a word of warning to her, jumped for shore, pulling her along with him.

Her landing was anything but graceful, for the rocks were wet and slippery and there was no substantial vegetation close by to offer even a precarious handhold. For the first few seconds Rosalind teetered, fighting to maintain her balance. If Brad had not held on to her, she might well have toppled back into the water. Fortunately, she avoided that particular mishap.

It was fortunate, indeed, for all too soon she had reason to be grateful that she had not gotten her boots wet.

Chapter Twelve

How much longer before we stop?

Rosalind had asked herself that question twenty times in the last hour, but she was not brave enough to ask it of Brad. He had told her the trip would be too difficult for her, and he had been correct, but she would fall over dead in her tracks before she admitted that fact to him.

If only she could rest for a time. And remove those retched boots! Nine of her toes were screaming in agony, while the tenth—much smaller than his fellows—had given up the ghost at least a mile back. At the moment, he was probably sitting in toe paradise celebrating his early demise.

When they left the *barco rabelo,* Brad had said they were at least three quarters of the way to the site of the prison camp. Unfortunately, their mustached captain could not, or would not, take them any farther up the Douro. Instead, he had told Brad of a small fishing village some five miles upriver, assuring him that for a price one of the fishermen would take them as far as it was possible to journey by water. Since the alternative was to walk thirty miles over the mountains, they chose to seek the fishermen and his village.

The moon was already high in the sky when they smelled the smoke of the cook fires and heard the sound of a baby crying. A minute later they were in the middle of the village—if one could call it that. The entire expanse of land was little more than a flat, open space between the foothills and the water. The village was improved by nothing more than five single-room houses huddled close together, and a wooden dock where three small fishing boats were tied up for the night.

"Doa noite!" Brad called into the darkness.

Rosalind thought that a rather odd way to announce their presence, but it seemed to do the trick. Almost immediately, a skinny little man with a shock of gray hair stuck his head out the door of one of the houses.

"Miguel!" the man shouted. "Pablo! *Venha!*"

Immediately two more men stepped out of nearby houses. They were much younger than the first man, and though they were not nearly as tall as Brad, they were stockily built. One of them looked as though he could knock over a tree with his bare fists. As they came closer, moving slowly and cautiously, Brad dropped the satchel to the ground and held his hands out, palms up, to show that he held no weapon.

In a quick, unintimidated spate of Portuguese, he explained that he was looking for someone to take him upriver. The fishermen looked at one another, silently seeking a meeting of the minds. Apparently they agreed to suspended suspicion for the moment, for the gray-haired man turned back toward the little house from which he had come, motioning for them to follow.

All of them filed into the single room. Aside from a rickety wooden table and two chairs, the only other furnishings were a baby's cradle and an old dresser piled high with what appeared to be the entire possessions— personal and domestic—of the household. A straw-filled mattress lay on the floor in the corner farthest from the fireplace, and seated cross-legged on the pallet was a pretty, dark-eyed young woman in a faded blue dress. A silken-haired baby perhaps two months old suckled contentedly at her breast.

Their host seated himself in one of the chairs and offered the other to Brad, while everyone else more or less leaned against any spare wall space. Rosalind would have liked to sit down and remove her boots, but she had not been invited to do so. Unaware of the protocol prevailing in such situations, she did not wish to offend anyone's sensibilities.

Brad did most of the talking, and though Rosalind understood none of the conversation, she could tell from the wariness in the gray-haired man's eyes that he wanted no part of them or their travel difficulties. One of the younger men, Miguel, showed some interest, but when he would have spoken to Brad, their host stilled him with a fierce look.

Into the silence that followed, the young woman with the baby spoke, surprising everyone in the room into turning to stare at her. *"Senhor,"* she said quietly.

"Senhora?" Brad replied, his tone respectful, as though he addressed a duchess.

Whatever she wished to ask, the young woman did not allow the gray-haired man's outraged glare to dissuade her. Instead, she posed a question to Brad, then waited for his reply.

"Sim, senhora," he said. "Joao Duarte."

A chorus of sighs sounded in the room, and the young woman smiled then pointed to the silken-haired baby who had fallen to sleep. It was only later that Rosalind learned the baby was the son of Joao Duarte, one of the *junta* leaders Brad had contacted before he was captured by the French. Duarte had obviously spoken of their meeting to his wife.

Acquaintance with Duarte, it appeared, was the letter of introduction needed in the village, and immediately Rosalind and Brad were accepted as honored guests. When their host excavated a bottle of port wine from the back of the dresser, the men all gathered around the table, their sun-bronzed faces now wreathed in smiles. They sat for what seemed hours, sipping wine and talking like old friends, presumably planning for the trip upriver on the morrow.

At some point during the planning, Rosalind sat down near the fireplace, with her knees pulled up to her chest and her head resting on her arms, and promptly fell asleep. When and how she came to be in one of the other houses, she did not know, but during the early morning hours, when the sky was beginning to turn from black to gray and hints of light filtered through the small window, she awoke to find herself on a pallet. Her spine was flush with the wall, and her face was snuggled against a broad, muscular back.

She did not need the pale light to know the man beside her was Brad. No more than she needed an explanation as to why they were sleeping thus—side by side, with both of them fully clothed. This was his way of shielding her from any unexpected encounters with the other males.

Soft snores sounded from the far side of the room, so Rosalind knew they were not alone. With Brad's tall physique acting as a buffer, there was no possibility of anyone inadvertently drawing too close to her. It was comforting to know that Brad protected her even while she slept.

It was also wildly exciting.

Yesterday on the boat she had wanted to touch him, to feel the muscles in his back ripple beneath her fingers, and now he was beside her, the warmth of his body keeping out the early morning chill. She could not help herself. She touched him.

Gently, so she did not wake him, Rosalind laid the palm of her hand just above his shoulder blade, then slowly, cautiously she smoothed her hand up to his shoulder. The muscles did not ripple as before, but she fancied they knew she was admiring them. They were sleeping, but very much alive to her touch.

Emboldened, she eased her hand down his arm, hesitating a moment to curl her fingers around his hard bicep. With her heart beating madly at the wondrous feel of him, she continued her exploration down his solid forearm to his wrist. When her fingertips encountered the soft, silky hair just beneath the cuff of his sleeve, she caught her breath.

He was so strong, so perfectly formed, and Rosalind wished with all her heart that he would turn and wrap those strong arms around her. He did not, of course, and after a time, when the pleasure of touching him became torment, she drew her hand away and eased up onto her knees, then to her feet.

Carefully she stepped over him and went outside, not pausing until she was on the wooden dock where the three boats were tied. There she remained, gazing into the water, until the sun drew pink streaks across the sky and the people of the village rose and began their daily tasks.

Brad had known when she awoke. He had been only half asleep, and when she first stirred, he came awake on the instant, painfully aware of her proximity, her soft body so close to his it nearly drove him wild. He could feel her warm breath upon his neck. When she first lifted her hand and touched his back, he was obliged to grit his teeth to keep from moaning. Then she slid her hand up to his shoulder, making his muscles cry out to respond to her caress.

Somehow he remained still. Even when her fingers molded around his bicep, heating his blood almost to the boiling point, he remained steadfast. It was when she slid her hand along his forearm that he was almost undone. Her fingertips touched the hair at his wrist and she caught her breath. The sound was like a love song, calling to him, begging him to turn and take her in his arms.

He was imagining himself holding her close, feeling her soft, pliant lips beneath his, when she eased away from him and got quietly to her feet. She stepped over him, and he was torn between catching her and pulling her back down beside him or letting her leave. Thankfully, he remembered in time that they were not alone, and he let her go. It was the most difficult thing he had ever done.

* * *

The morning was fresh and cool, with the dew still glistening upon the rocks at the water's edge when Brad and Rosalind climbed into Miguel's fishing boat. They had broken their fast at the gray-haired man's home, and his daughter had served them warm, crusty bread and chucks of spicy fish. While the men talked over cups of thick, black coffee, the daughter stepped out of the room. Almost as soon as she left, her baby woke and began to fret.

Rosalind was near the cradle, so without thinking what a young boy would do under the circumstances, she picked up the infant and held him in her arms. While she patted him on the back and made little cooing noises to comfort him, she nuzzled her cheek against his head, enjoying his new-baby sweetness.

If she had suddenly grown horns and run screaming into the river, she could not have brought more attention to herself. All conversation ceased, and both Miguel and the gray-haired man stared at her, their mouths agape. Instantly, they both looked away, embarrassment turning their faces from tan to copper, and only then did Rosalind remember that she was dressed as a scruffy lad.

Afraid Brad would be angry with her for making herself conspicuous, she shot a glance his way. Like the other men, he was staring at her, but his expression had nothing to do with embarrassment. Though what it had to do with, Rosalind could not say.

Oddly enough, his blue eyes appeared softer than she had ever seen them before, and if she had not known better, she would have said he was awed by what he saw. Though why he should be awed by the sight of her holding a baby, she could not say. She had held dozens of infants in her lifetime, and no man had ever looked at her like that before.

As it transpired, she had little time to ponder Brad's reaction, for the mother returned at that moment and came immediately to retrieve her child. *"Obrigado,"* she said shyly.

The young woman's entrance seemed to break the silence that had fallen upon the room, and the three men rose from the table. It was left to Brad to thank their hostess for her hospitality, and while he spoke with her, Rosalind made her escape from the house. She walked rather self-consciously to the dock, her gaze concentrated upon her booted feet, and she did not look up again until Brad joined her, followed by Miguel.

Without saying a word, Brad gave her a gentle nudge toward the boat. It was a small craft, obviously meant to accommodate two fishermen, and it rocked precariously when she climbed aboard. If it had pitched her headfirst into the water, however, Rosalind would not have cried out. She had made enough of a spectacle of herself for one day. After taking her place in the bow, she swore a silent oath to be like the air they breathed, necessary for survival but invisible. She kept that oath, too. At least for the first two hours.

When Rosalind had first spied Miguel the evening before, she had decided he was the most powerfully built man she had ever seen, imagining him capable of felling trees with his bare hands. His performance in the boat only reinforced that opinion, for he manned the oars with the strength of two men, rowing with speed and apparent ease.

Brad posed a question to him several times during the first two hours of their journey, and each time the answer had been, *"Não senhor."* When he asked the question again, however, Miguel answered in the affirmative.

To Rosalind's surprise, Miguel lifted the oars out of the water, resting them inside the boat. Then the two men stood, making the boat rock with their combined weights. Moving carefully, so as not to tip the craft, they exchanged places, with Miguel in the stern and Brad manning the oars.

Brad was a strong man, and he rowed with the grace of the natural athlete, but he was unable to match Miguel's strength or maintain the rapid pace the fisherman had set. After perhaps half an hour, Rosalind noticed that Brad's breathing was audible, and when she touched his knee, obliging him to look up from beneath the slouchy-brimmed hat, she saw that his upper lip was covered in perspiration and his skin had a slightly ashen cast.

At the sight of him, her heart lodged in her throat. "I knew this would happen," she said, totally forgetting her vow of silence. "You have pushed yourself beyond your limit, and now you are ill."

He glared at her as though he would like to argue the point, but after several moments of staring—moments in which neither of them backed down—Brad nodded as if acknowledging the truth of the situation. Without a word, he lifted the oars out of the water.

Miguel rowed the final few miles, and when they found a likely spot to come ashore, he pulled the boat up onto the riverbank, as though he did not mean to return to the village right away. The conversation that passed between the two men following this act was somewhat heated, but in time Brad thanked him and they shook hands.

"What has happened?" Rosalind asked. No point in keeping quiet now. Miguel had already heard her speak, so he knew she was not Portuguese, and if he had questions about her gender, he was too polite to ask them. Instead, he waited quietly while Brad explained the situation to her.

"Rather than return to the village where he would not be connected with this day's activities, Miguel has chosen to deal himself into our little card game."

Rosalind could not stop her sigh of relief. She looked at the fisherman, silently thanking him for his assistance.

"He knows where the prison camp is located," Brad added. "Furthermore, he does not like the soldiers. It seems they have appropriated his entire catch more than once, leaving his little family without food for the next day.

"Miguel also informs me that the soldiers are nervous because of the recent victories by the English, and he has convinced me that his presence here is less likely to cause suspicion than mine. For that reason, he proposes to act as an intermediary in our attempt to purchase Ashford's release."

Brad smiled then, but it was not mirth Rosalind saw, it was chagrin.

"Miguel is a good man," he said, "and I believe that he, like you, is concerned for my health. He thinks I cannot walk six miles over rough terrain."

Six miles! Rosalind's blistered feet rebelled at the very thought. "Does he speak French?"

"He knows a few phrases. Those who are overrun

by a conquering army are often obliged to learn the language of the conqueror. Therefore," he continued, "I have agreed to let him go in my stead to try to negotiate Ashford's release."

"And if he cannot negotiate it? What then?"

"In that event, he is to see if he can bribe someone into giving Ashford a message from me—a message informing him that I will meet him at midnight tonight, in that spot where I was shot."

Rosalind could not still the tremor in her voice. "Please tell me you do not mean to help him escape. That is far too dangerous. It is how you were shot in the first—"

Brad reached out and squeezed her hand. "It is merely an alternate plan. Hopefully it will not come to that."

"And . . . and if it does?"

He let go her hand and straightened. "Let us not worry over something that may never happen. First we will see what my money can buy."

Rosalind turned to the fisherman, and though they exchanged not a word, it was as though a common concern passed between them.

Turning back to Brad, she said, "Tell Miguel that I wish him Godspeed."

She supposed Brad did as she asked. In any event, he said something, then he removed a leather pouch from his satchel. After pouring the contents on the ground, revealing an astonishing number of gold coins, he gathered up the coins, returned them to the pouch, and handed the whole to Miguel.

The fisherman's hands trembled as he put a sum that must have appeared to him a king's ransom inside his shirt. The money stowed, he turned northward and began walking toward the mountains. He did not return until dusk.

Brad and Rosalind waited at the water's edge, thinking to guard the fishing boat from anyone who might happen by. After a couple of hours, however, Brad suggested they find a sheltered place in the rocks, some place out of the sun. "You must be hot," he said, "I know I am."

Actually, Rosalind felt chilled from sitting on the damp ground, and it was only because of the sun's rays that she had managed to keep her teeth from chattering. Suddenly suspicious, she reached over and touched Brad's forehead. It was like an oven on baking day. "Brad! You have a fever."

"Nonsense. I am merely warm from the sun."

She did not argue with him, but later in the afternoon, when he began to shiver, she could no longer hide her fear. A riverbank not six miles from an enemy prison camp was no place to be ill. This was the reason she had insisted on coming with him; she had been afraid he might have a relapse.

When she felt his head again, and it was even hotter than before, Brad admitted that he felt unwell. He insisted that a little rest was all he needed. "A few minutes sleep, and I will be as good as new."

It spoke volumes that he allowed her to arrange the satchel so he could use it for a pillow, then he laid down and closed his eyes. Some time later, when Rosalind removed her jacket and placed it across his shoulders, he did not even stir.

Chapter Thirteen

At dusk, when Miguel returned, big with excitement, Brad still slept. All afternoon he had alternated between shivering and burning up, and now when the fisherman tried to wake him by shaking his shoulder, Brad's only response was a moan.

Rosalind and Miguel stood about helplessly, neither knowing what was best to do. Feeling she must do something, however, Rosalind employed the universal witlessness of those who try to communicate to someone in a language they do not understand—she spoke slowly, carefully enunciating the English words. "What . . . happened . . . at . . . the . . . prison . . . camp?"

The fisherman merely stared at her, then he employed the universally witless response by telling a long and apparently complicated tale in his native tongue—a story he emphasized with a great deal of gesturing and hand waving. At the end of his story, obviously suffering from the delusion that he had communicated his thoughts, he caught hold of Rosalind's arm and began urging her in the direction from which he had come.

"*Venha,*" he said.

Rosalind had heard the word often enough to know that it was a request for her to come with him, but she had no intention of leaving Brad.

"*Venha,*" the man said again.

"*Não,*" she replied, pulling away from his grasp. "I will not go any place without the *senhor.*" She pointed to Brad, who lay shivering beneath her jacket. "He is ill."

Apparently understanding her wish to remain with Brad, Miguel looked all about him, as if hoping to see help arrive from some heretofore unexpected source. When assistance was not forthcoming, he turned back to Rosalind. After speaking slowly, as she had done, and with similar results, he pointed to himself, then to her, and finally toward the mountains. "*Venha,*" he said again.

Not finished with his plea, he pointed to her mouth, made talking signs with his fingers, and said something that sounded like "English."

At last she understood. He needed her to come with him because she spoke English.

Miguel had returned alone, so it was apparent he had been unable to purchase a release for Lieutenant Ashford. That being true, he had probably followed Brad's alternate plan and bribed a guard to deliver a message to the lieutenant. Now, of course, Ashford would be expecting to meet Brad at the designated spot, wherever that might be.

Rosalind remembered Brad's account of their attempted escape, but all she knew was that they had tried to climb out of the moat. Chances were he had not told even that much to the fisherman.

The situation grew more complicated by the minute.

George Ashford would be waiting at some specific spot, expecting to meet Brad, and even if Miguel was fortunate enough to find that spot, he would be unable to communicate instructions to the Englishman. It was doubtful if he would be able to convince the lieutenant that he was to be trusted, and that he had come to help him escape. Ashford might think it was a trap of some sort and balk, thereby risking both their lives.

Rosalind closed her eyes, not wanting to be responsible for making this decision. On one hand, Miguel needed someone who could explain to Ashford who they were and why they had come. On the other hand, she could not—would not—leave the man she loved alone and defenseless. Anything might happen to him.

"Não," she said again. "I will not come with you. Besides, my feet are in bad shape. I doubt I could walk six yards, never mind six miles."

There was a look of desperation in Miguel's dark eyes, but he seemed to be trying to understand what she was saying. Remembering that a picture was worth a thousand words, Rosalind sat down and removed one boot and stocking, showing him her blistered feet. "Sore," she said. "I cannot walk over the mountains. I am awfully sorry, but there it is."

"Ahh," the fisherman said, examining the angry spots on her heels and toes then nodding his understanding of her predicament.

Glad to have at least one thing settled, Rosalind slipped the stocking and boot back on her foot. Miguel waited respectfully while she donned the shoe, and as she attempted to get to her feet, he extended his large hand to assist her.

Not wanting to be churlish, especially now the matter was all settled, she took the proffered hand. To her surprise, the fisherman did more than help her to her feet. One minute she was being assisted off the ground and the next she was being lifted into the air and tossed like a sack of wheat over a very broad shoulder.

"Stop!" she yelled. "You cannot do this. I—I must remain here. Brad needs me."

Unfortunately, her words were wasted on Miguel, who was already headed north, toward the mountains.

The moon came out full and bright, aiding them with its yellow-white light. They did not actually go all the way to the mountains, but remained in the foothills. Even so, the terrain was every bit as rugged as Brad had predicted, and it would have been twice as treacherous if they had been obliged to travel in the dark.

As Miguel climbed one craggy outcropping after another, he moved with the same unflagging strength he had exhibited while rowing. If it slowed him down to have a female of perhaps nine stone on his shoulder, he showed no evidence of the fact. Rosalind had argued with him for the first mile or so, trying to say something—anything—to convince him to set her down. Nothing worked. It was probably just as well, for she doubted she could have climbed without mishap.

When he stopped once and shushed her, then whispered something that sounded like a warning, she remembered they were headed toward who knew how many French soldiers, enemies of herself and her country. After that, she did not utter another sound.

The climbing went on for fully two hours, with Rosalind thinking they would never reach the camp. Miguel finally stopped just behind a group of large boulders and set her on her feet. She was obliged to hold on to one of the huge rocks until her head ceased to spin and the world righted itself, but as soon as she had her balance, she peeped out at the clearing up ahead. As Brad had told her, the prison camp was a makeshift affair of tents and lean-tos set up on several acres of leveled farmland, and it was surrounded by a dry moat at least fifteen feet deep and twenty feet wide.

Rosalind gasped when she saw the camp, for it was larger and more crowded with prisoners than she had imagined. And the moat appeared quite formidable. Furthermore, with the moon so bright, no one could climb in and out of that monstrous ditch without being seen by at least one of the French soldiers who patrolled the perimeter. She watched them now as they walked back and forth, each soldier guarding an area perhaps four hundred yards long.

She shivered at her first look at the enemy. They were a ragtag-looking group, but they were armed, with their rifles on their shoulders and their bayonets fixed. Frightened and angry beyond belief, Rosalind wanted to weep, for she and Brad had come to Portugal on a fool's errand. Escape from this place was impossible. As for detection and sudden death by gunshot, that seemed imminently possible.

No, it was unavoidable.

She had no more than admitted the futility of an attempted escape when the fisherman tapped her on the shoulder and pointed off to their right where two men were moving toward the moat, crawling like snakes upon their bellies. Rosalind held her breath, for a

French guard was walking straight toward the men, and it was inconceivable that he would not see them and open fire. To her immense relief, the guard did a crisp about-face and began to walk in the opposite direction; at the same time, the two men slipped over the edge of the moat and slid down the side.

When Miguel nudged her arm and muttered, *"Venha,"* Rosalind could not imagine what he wanted her to do. All too quickly his purpose became apparent, however. He intended to go to the aid of those men in the moat, and he meant for her to come along. Out in the open. In the moonlight. With armed Frenchmen all around.

Rosalind would have yelled her protest, but her voice failed her. The words seemed to stick in her throat, and while Miguel held her wrist, pulling her after him as he moved from the concealment of one boulder to another, she tried to tell him she could not go. She was too frightened.

She was no hero. She belonged back in England, in the safety of her parents' home. She should not be in this appalling place, dressed in boy's clothes, but in a warm house, wearing lace caps and looking after her sisters' children, fulfilling her destiny as the spinster aunt.

Sick with fear, she thought of Brad, recalling how brave he had been. He had been shot trying to stop the guard from killing Ashford, and now he was back at the river, ill once again as a result of trying to bring about the lieutenant's rescue. He was a real hero. Not like her. She was too frightened to be a hero.

Then suddenly, almost as though she were a puppet and someone else was pulling the strings, Rosalind found herself on her stomach, crawling as she had seen the two men crawl. The fisherman led the way, but she followed close behind him, dirt in her mouth and a sea of perspiration running into her eyes, heading toward that horrendous ditch.

They reached the rim of the moat and looked over. The two men were there, one blond and slender, the other a burly fellow who looked as if he could match Miguel in the art of uprooting trees with his bare hands. Swallowing with difficulty, Rosalind said, "Hsst. Ashford. Over here."

In an instant the two men were below her, with the slender one busily climbing up on the burly fellow's shoulders. Miguel seemed to know what was needed, and he pushed her aside and reached down to catch the slender man's wrists. In less time than it took to blink the perspiration from her eyes, the man was up and over the rim, lying beside her, his breath coming in deep, ragged gasps.

He rested only a second or two before turning onto his stomach to help Miguel pull the big fellow up and over. The second rescue was not as easy as the first, and while they struggled to pull the much heavier man up, Rosalind looked across at the enemy soldier, who was once again turned in their direction.

"Shh," she said. "The guard is coming."

At her warning, the men stopped, remaining quite still, their heads down, with the big one hanging halfway up the side of the moat.

Rosalind held her breath, watching the guard walk ever closer, until he was scarcely fifty yards away from them. The moonlight shone brightly, illuminating the moat and all four of them. It was impossible for the guard not to see them, and at any moment she expected to feel bullets whizzing past her head. At least, she hoped they whizzed past!

Heaven help her, she wanted nothing so much as to jump up and run away. But she did not. She could not run and draw attention to the three men, leaving them targets for the Frenchman's bullets.

Trembling all over, she thought she could not endure the torment of fear another moment, and yet she did. Biting her bottom lip until she tasted blood, she prayed as she had never prayed before. She prayed for the lives of these three brave men, and she prayed for Brad, who was a hero and deserved to have his conscience free of guilt about having been sent home in Lieutenant Ashford's place.

And please God, do not let the Frenchman see us.

Whether it was divine intervention or the power of Brad's gold, Rosalind neither knew nor cared, but she thanked them both when the guard turned and walked back in the opposite direction.

Once he was out of hearing, she said, "Quickly."

Miguel and Lieutenant Ashford seemed to double their efforts, and within a matter of seconds, the third man was up and over the rim of the moat.

"This way," she said, and without further conversation, the four of them crawled with all speed toward the safety of the boulders. They were well out of range of the bullets when the Frenchman set up a cry.

"Arrête!" he yelled, and fired his rifle. They got to their feet and ran just the same, not stopping until they were at least half a mile into the foothills.

* * *

"Please, lad," George Ashford asked when they stopped for a few moments' rest, "will you tell us to whom we are indebted for our rescue?"

They had all fallen to the ground, their breathing labored. All, that is, except for the fisherman, who walked back a way to be certain they were not being followed.

Ashford and the Sergeant Major had shown signs of fatigue early on, and Rosalind remembered that they had been without proper nourishment for the past seven months. To keep them from pushing themselves beyond their limits, she had claimed that it was she who needed the frequent stops. Actually, she wanted nothing more than to hurry back to Brad, for she was worried about his condition.

"To answer your question, Lieutenant, you owe your rescue to Brad Stone."

"By jingo," the Sergeant Major said. "When that Frenchy guard give me the message, I thought surely I'd misheard him. I never figured to glim me eyes on Stone again."

Rosalind bristled, almost as if the man had offered an insult to her beloved. "Brad returned to Portugal as soon as he had completed his mission, for he could not abide the thought of Lieutenant Ashford languishing in that prison camp when it was *his* freedom that had been purchased, and not Brad's."

"And you came with him?" Ashford asked. "You were very brave."

"Here, here," the Sergeant Major agreed, "showed real bottom, you did. And you nothing but a halfling. What be your name, lad?"

Not wanting to answer, she said, "It is Brad who is brave."

"True enough," Ashford said. "Where is Stone now?"

While she explained that Brad had overdone and suffered a relapse, Miguel returned and squatted down beside her. To her surprise, he touched one of her boots then patted his shoulder.

"No, no," she said, realizing what he was asking, "I can walk. Truly, I do not need to be—"

He either could not or would not understand her, for before she could finish her plea, he had hoisted her up and slung her over his shoulder once again.

"See here, old fellow," Ashford said, embarrassment making his voice a bit strident, "I've no wish to appear ungrateful for your rescue, but I do not believe the lad wants a lift."

"Save your breath," Rosalind said. "Argument is futile, for he does not understand a word of English. Besides, though you may find this hard to credit, Miguel is being chivalrous."

The lieutenant took her at her word and said no more; he merely fell into step behind the fisherman and his passenger. With frequent stops necessary, their progress was slow, and by the time they arrived at the water's edge, the moon had begun to wane and the promise of morning showed in the faint graying of the still-dark sky.

Brad lay where they had left him, but he had thrown off Rosalind's jacket. When she touched his shoulder he looked up at her through fever-dulled eyes. "Brad," she whispered, "we have returned. Ashford is with us, and we can all go home now."

As it turned out, going home was not to be that easy. When the five of them were all crammed into Miguel's small boat, it began to take on water from their combined weights. Immediately, Ashford jumped out, landing with a splash in the cold river. "It will not hold us all," he said. "Someone must remain behind."

His words hung in the air for several moments, then he said, "If you will point me in the right direction, lad, I will walk to the village."

"No, sir," the Sergeant Major said, jumping into the water as well. "You get back in the boat, Lieutenant. I have been cooped up in that place a long time. A good walk is just what I need."

"You will both go in the boat," Rosalind said, surprising herself as much as them.

"Nay, lad," Ashford began, "you have been as brave a youngster as I ever hope to see, but I cannot allow you to—"

"Say no more!" she commanded. "We will do this my way, and I want no argument about it. If the French soldiers should find you, they will take you back to the prison camp. They are not looking for a sick man and a boy. You and the Sergeant Major will return to the village with Miguel, then he can come back for Brad and me."

"But, my boy, we cannot let you do that."

Rosalind's back stiffened, and when she spoke, her tone was soft but emphatic. "You have no say in the matter, Lieutenant. The decision is entirely mine."

"But the man is ill and—"

"He was ill before," she said. "I applaud your motive in sending Brad home in your place the first time. Such gallantry did you credit, and I honestly believe you saved his life. However, your unselfishness left him with a debt of honor that weighed heavily upon his conscience—a debt he came all the way back to Portugal to repay. Now you would sacrifice yourself for him again? No, sir, you will not. I will not allow you to do that to him a second time."

Rosalind stood upon a large flat rock at the water's edge and watched the fishing boat until it grew so small she could no longer distinguish it from the ripples in the river. Then she returned to the spot where Miguel and the Sergeant Major had carried Brad. His eyes were open, but his face was still quite warm.

Exhausted both mentally and physically, Rosalind lay down beside the man she loved, getting as close to him as possible, seeking warmth and solace from his nearness. As if he knew what she needed, Brad put his arm around her waist and drew her closer still, her back against his chest. Their bodies fit perfectly, and it felt wonderful to be in his arms.

"So," he said, his voice husky from sleep and fever, "Ashford is safe at last."

"Yes. The lieutenant is safe and on his way home."

"You must be very happy."

"I am now," she said. Taking Brad's wrist, she pulled his arm up across her chest and held his palm against her lips for a moment; then she tucked his hand beneath her cheek and used it for a pillow, snuggling close in his embrace. "Very happy."

And then she slept.

Miguel and the gray-haired man found them there late that afternoon, still wrapped in one another's arms.

Chapter Fourteen

The next two and a half weeks passed in a haze for Rosalind. She and Brad spent two nights at the fishing village, until his fever abated and he declared himself fit to travel. Then Miguel took the two of them in his boat to meet the *barco rabelo* as it made its way back east to Oporto to deliver more barrels of wine to the caves.

Brad tried to press Miguel into accepting some of the remaining gold coins, but the fisherman refused to take them. Finally, after much argument, Brad put his money away and shook Miguel's hand, thanking him for all he had done for them.

When the men had said their goodbyes, the fisherman turned to Rosalind, who still wore her young-boy garb.

"I wish I knew how to thank you," she said. "Without your help, we might all have perished." She knew he did not understand a word she said, but she had needed to say it just the same. It was time to leave, so she reached out her hand to him. *"Obrigado,* Miguel."

Taking her proffered hand, the man who had slung her over his shoulder like a sack of wheat made her a very courtly bow; then he lifted her fingers to his lips for a brief salute. Speaking very slowly and precisely, he said, "Very welcome, *senhora.*"

Senhora. Rosalind gasped. When had the fisherman discovered her deception? And did the other villagers know of it as well? It was a question whose answer she would never know.

The captain of the *barco rabelo,* that same teak-faced fellow with the impressive mustache, seemed not to suspect that she was female. He took them aboard his sailboat without showing the least interest in her gender.

On the return journey to Oporto, the boat required a combination of sail and oars. Consequently, the trip down the *Douro Rio* took them almost ten hours. When they arrived, Brad went immediately to the docks and secured passage to Portsmouth for Rosalind for the next morning. He, on the other hand, claimed he needed to remain in Oporto for a few days, to see if he could do anything for Ashford and the Sergeant Major, who had reported to the nearest military unit.

No matter how Rosalind protested that she should remain behind as well, Brad would not hear her. He insisted that she return on the morrow, and in time she relented. She had no other choice. From the way Brad had treated her since his recovery—with extreme politeness, as though they were no more than casual acquaintances—it was obvious he was weary of the responsibility of protecting her. As well, because he was now safe and would be returning on the next frigate, *she* no longer had a reason to protect him. Therefore, there was no point in her staying.

It broke her heart to leave him, but what could she

do? Though still posing as a lad, she was too despondent to wish for company, so she remained in her cabin the entire voyage. She emerged only when the frigate docked in Portsmouth and the captain came to tell her Brad had asked him to escort her to Sussex.

The nice old gentleman tried to entertain her on the short ride to Bilchester, but Rosalind would not be cheered—not even by her first glimpse of Stoneleigh Park, Brad's lovely old mellowed brick and mortar home in Sussex. The rolling green downs were especially beautiful after two weeks at sea, but even their beauty was not sufficient to ease the pain in her heart.

"Rosalind! Oh, my dear girl," Lady Sizemore cried when her niece entered the pretty pink guest bedchamber her ladyship had been occupying for the past five weeks. "I cannot believe you are here at last."

"Believe it, Aunt Eudora, for I am returned."

The teary-eyed lady pulled Rosalind into an enthusiastic embrace. "You cannot know how I suffered that next morning at the Old Ship Inn when I discovered you had disappeared once again. Then to be told by Lady Browne that Clotilde, that dreadful maid she employs, had aided you to stow away on some frigate . . ." She placed her hand on her ample bosom, "I vow, my heart threatened to fail me that very instant. To think of you on a frigate bound for Portugal, alone and unchaperoned."

"Not alone, Aunt, for I was—"

"I am persuaded I would have gone into a decline had Lady Browne not offered me sanctuary here at Stoneleigh Park."

"Sanctuary? Surely that is a bit dramatic, Aunt. You had no need for refuge."

Lady Sizemore straightened, giving her niece a very

haughty look. "Did I not? I presume you thought I would just whisk myself back to Oxfordshire without you."

Actually, Rosalind had not given any thought at all to what her aunt might do, but she could hardly say that to the lady.

"How was I to face your parents?" Eudora Sizemore continued. "What was I to tell them? You give me more credit than I deserve, if you believe me capable of facing your mother and telling her that her oldest daughter had gone off to some war-ravaged country with a gentleman she had already refused to marry." She shook her head. "No, I tell you. I am not so brave as all that. Nor am I—"

The diatribe was halted mid-sentence, for Rosalind chose that moment to remove her cap, exposing the short curls that hugged her head.

"Rosalind!" Lady Sizemore screamed. "Your hair! Dear girl, what have you done?" The lady moaned, dropping into a rose satin chaise lounge and calling for her sal volatile. "Heaven preserve me," she said, waving the smelling salts beneath her nose, "your mother will never speak to me again!"

Rosalind tossed *The Times* she had been reading onto the petit point settee. "Yes," she replied to her mother's inquiry, "I am ready. Only let me run up to my bedchamber and fetch my bonnet."

She had been back in Whitstock for less than a month, and already she had made enough visits and drunk enough tea to last her a lifetime. And now she was off to her sister Caroline's to see if she could lift that lady's spirits.

"You must go," Mrs. Hinton had said earlier that morning, trying to turn Rosalind's negative answer into a positive one. "The last days before one's confinement are so tedious. And it is not as though you had anything better to do."

As if to substantiate her argument, she continued, "Just as your sister said when last we visited her, 'It is an indisputable fact that unmarried women never have anything important to occupy their time.' Ergo, they should be happy to accommodate any of their married relatives. Most especially if that relative is a sister."

Rosalind had finally relented and agreed to drive to the vicarage for the third time that week. "Excellent," Mrs. Hinton said. "And when we are there, Rosalind, pray, let us hear no more nonsense about forming a society to send parcels to prisoners of war. I vow, child, I do not know where you get such shabby-genteel notions. As though any proper young lady would concern herself with such unseemly matters."

"I can hardly credit, ma'am, that liniment and soap are unseemly."

"But you mentioned sending them other items. Delousing powers and—and drawers! 'Tis too farouche by half. I should not be able to hold my head up if it was known that a daughter of mine was sending strange men such disgusting items."

"I merely suggested, ma'am, that as the wife of a clergyman, Caroline might feel it her duty to head such a committee. Now that I have seen how opposed she is to the idea, I will not broach the subject to her again."

Rosalind had kept it to herself that she had already written a letter to General Sir Edward Jamison at the War Office asking his thoughts on the logistics of such an enterprise. In her letter she had suggested that the ladies who made up the parcels might also collect monies to pay for their delivery, citing as possible conveyers the empty *barco rabelos* that returned upriver almost daily.

She had not yet heard from Sir Edward, but Brad had said he was a good man, and that he could be trusted. If Brad trusted him, then Rosalind trusted him. She would wait to hear from the general.

Of course, if she were honest with herself, she would admit that the person she most wanted to hear from was Brad. Her heart ached each time the post was brought from Whitstock and she had no word from him. She knew he did not love her as she loved him, but he had said they must remain friends. And did friends not correspond?

"Rosalind," Mrs. Hinton said, breaking into her reverie, "your bonnet. I thought you said you were fetching it."

"Of course, Mother, I shall be but a minute."

As it turned out, she needed much more than a minute, for as she crossed the marble-tiled vestibule from the small sitting room, her destination the stairs, the knocker sounded at the front entrance. Because there did not seem to be any servants around at that moment, Rosalind opened the wide oak door herself.

To her surprise—nay, her horror!—Lieutenant George Ashford stood just outside. He wore a bright new uniform, and he held his shako beneath his arm. He looked marvelously fit and healthy, but he was the last person in the world she wished to see. If he should recognize her as the lad he knew in Portugal, who knew what repercussions might result.

"Miss Hinton?" he asked.

"Lieutenant!"

The gentleman made her a crisp bow. "You remember me then?"

"Of—of course," she replied.

"My uncle, Sir Miles Vernon, informs me that you and your aunt, Lady Sizemore, were so kind as to pay me a visit . . . or rather, you thought to pay me a visit, but it was not I whom you visited but . . ." He paused, becoming tangled in the peculiarities of the story. "What I mean to say is, I appreciate your thoughtfulness, and I wished to stop by and pay my respects. It was most kind of you, ma'am, to call upon a soldier home from the wars."

"Which I perceive you to be now, sir. Pray, allow me to welcome you home."

"Thank you, ma'am."

Common courtesy decreed that she invite him in, so she stepped back and opened wide the door. "Please, Lieutenant, will you not come in and allow me to present you to my mother?"

He entered the vestibule. "You are very good, ma'am. I—"

There was now but a foot or so distance between them, and while he looked at her face, a rather puzzled expression in his eyes, Rosalind reached up nervously to touch the satin-edged tippet to her cap. She had begun to wear lace caps since returning to her home, for she had found that they covered her shorn locks and did not occasion nearly as many questions.

"Forgive me for staring, Miss Hinton, but you look very familiar."

"As do you, sir. Surely your uncle told you that ours was an acquaintance made some eleven years ago, on the occasion of the wedding of my mother's cousin, Miss Henrietta Willoughby."

"Of course. Henrietta. Her brother and I were particular friends." His smile held a touch of boyish devilment. "We were used to call him, 'Stick,' on account of his knobby-knees."

"So I recall, sir. I met that gentleman at the same time I made your acquaintance."

He allowed her to show him to the small sitting room where her mother waited, and as might be expected, Mrs. Hinton was beside herself with pleasure that her unmarried daughter had such a personable caller.

"Lieutenant Ashford," the lady said, "you are most welcome, sir. Though I was unaware that you and my daughter were known to one another, I am delighted to make your acquaintance."

When they were all seated, Mrs. Hinton asked their caller if he would take tea with them.

"Thank you, ma'am, I should like that. Since I returned from the peninsula, I seem unable to refuse food of any kind."

"I am not surprised," Mrs. Hinton said, "I daresay they do not know how to make a decent cup of tea in— Portugal was it? My daughter and I were just discussing that country. She feels great sympathy for the poor soldiers who are imprisoned there."

Rosalind realized that her mother had no way of knowing the appalling conditions prevailing in the prison camps, or that Ashford had been a prisoner, but she blushed for her all the same. As well, she felt compelled to offer the gentleman an apology. "Your pardon, sir, if . . ." she stopped, for Ashford was staring at her again, and this time his concentration was intense.

She knew the moment he realized who she was, for he caught his breath, the sound almost a gasp. To stop him blurting out something that would enlighten her mother as to her sojourn in Portugal, Rosalind said, "How—how pleased Sir Miles must be to have you home at last, Lieutenant."

Ashford obviously heard the trepidation in her voice, for he visibly suppressed his surprise at his very startling discovery. After breathing deeply, then exhaling, he said, "My uncle is very pleased at my safe return, Miss Hinton. As am I. I would be even more pleased, however, if I could offer my deep, and most heartfelt gratitude to the lad whose bravery made my escape possible."

Rosalind felt her cheeks blaze.

"A lad?" Mrs. Hinton asked.

"Yes, ma'am. He was a lad like no other, and if I should have him before me at this very moment, I would tell him that I shall never forget him. I am humbled by his valor. He is a hero in the very best sense of the word, and I should wish him to know that as long as I am alive in this world, I am his to command."

Chapter Fifteen

"Miss Hinton," Ashford said, once he had drunk his tea and announced his need to leave before he overstayed his welcome, "I believe we have a mutual friend."

"We do?"

"Yes, ma'am, and directly I leave here, I am scheduled to travel to the gentleman's home in Sussex. May I carry any messages for you to Lord Stone?"

Mrs. Hinton's eyes opened wide in surprise, and before she could demand to know how her daughter was acquainted with a peer, Rosalind said, "It is his lordship's grandmother, Lady Browne, with whom I claim acquaintance, Lieutenant. My aunt and I were her guests at Stoneleigh Park for several weeks in May and June. At that time, I believe, Lord Stone was in Portugal."

Ashford nodded, understanding her message. "A fine

fellow, Stone. Perhaps you will have an opportunity to meet him later."

Rosalind felt her heart pound just talking about Brad. "I cannot think it at all likely that Lord Stone and I shall ever meet, but if you will be so kind, sir, you may give my regards to his grandmother."

Ashford declared himself quite willing to relay the message. After saluting Mrs. Hinton's hand, then holding Rosalind's very tightly before taking it to his lips, he bowed smartly and bid them a good afternoon.

"Well," Mrs. Hinton said, once his horse was heard trotting down the carriageway, "that is a fine young man. How is it, my dear, that you have never mentioned him before?" Not giving her time to answer, she continued, "And why is it you failed to mention that this mysterious Lady Browne, at whose home you were a guest for such an unconscionably long time, has a grandson?"

Rosalind was forced to swallow the tears that threatened to obstruct her throat. "I did not mention him, Mama, because he is not now, nor will he ever be, a part of my life."

With that she excused herself to fetch her bonnet. "For I am persuaded Caroline will think we have forgotten her. And you know how it upsets her to expect a visit at a certain time only to have others be unpunctual."

"My, yes," her mother replied, "she is so easily provoked these days. Do hurry," she called after Rosalind's retreating form, "we must not keep your sister waiting, for she is bound to say we did it just to vex her."

Lieutenant Ashford's visit that next week to Stoneleigh Park did not so much *vex* Lord Stone as it put him in a frightful temper—the kind of temper, his grandmother informed him, reminiscent of a bear following a baiting.

"What in heaven's name is wrong with you?" she asked the morning after the lieutenant's arrival. "I thought you liked that young man."

"I do," Brad insisted, turning from the drawing room window and his contemplation of the distant downs with their dotting of cloud-white sheep. "It is quite possible that I owe him my life."

"And that, of course, is why you treated him in such a churlish manner last evening. Gratitude."

Brad crossed the pale maroon and yellow carpet to join his grandmother on the gold settee. Taking her hand in his, he said, "Forgive me, ma'am. I am a bit out of sorts lately."

"I had noticed as much. As I recall, the malady came upon you when you arrived at Stoneleigh and found a certain adventurous young lady no longer in residence. Now, for some strange reason, the lieutenant's coming seems to have exacerbated the condition."

"You overstate the case, Grandmother."

"Not a bit of it. Why, when the lieutenant was so kind as to relay to me a message from my dear Rosalind, you practically snarled at the man." She studied a slight imperfection in the blond lace at her sleeve, and while she examined it, she said, oh so casually, "If I did not know better, my boy, I would say you were jealous of that young man."

"Jealous? Me? Why, I—" Brad started to deny the accusation, then thought better of it. "Can you blame me for my feelings, ma'am, when he is the most fortunate of men? When he possesses the one thing in the world I want with all my heart?"

"And what is that?"

"Rosalind's love."

"Lummox!" declared his doting grandmother. "Have you lost your senses? Rosalind does not love him."

Brad took the name-calling in good part, but he was obliged to correct her ladyship's misconception. "Do you know why Rosalind risked her reputation, her very life even, to accompany me to Portugal?"

"Yes," she replied. "Do you?"

"Of course. It was to save George Ashford."

The diminutive lady rolled her eyes heavenward. "And where did you get such a preposterous idea?"

"She told me."

"I do not believe it!"

"You would, ma'am, if you had seen how happy she was once Ashford was rescued."

By chance, the gentleman under discussion chose that moment to enter the room, a smile upon his handsome face. "Ah, Lieutenant," Lady Browne greeted him, "do come join us. My grandson was just relating to me a most interesting *on-dit* concerning your future happiness."

The smile on George Ashford's face definitely wavered. *"My* happiness, ma'am?"

"Certainly, sir. Brad tells me you have won the heart of a very special young lady, and if that is true, allow me to be the first to wish you happy."

"A young lady?" he repeated. The gentleman's Adam's apple bobbed as he swallowed something that seemed to be impeding his breathing. "There must be some mistake, Lady Browne, for I have only just returned from the peninsula. I do not yet number any young ladies among my acquaintance. As for wishing me happy, I assure you, such felicitations are premature, as I have no plans for settling down in the near future."

Brad stared coldly at his guest, his eyes tossing razor-sharp knives at the young man. "Devil take it, Ashford, would you have us believe you do not know Miss Rosalind Hinton? That there is not an understanding between the two of you?"

Their visitor looked as though he wished he had remained another hour in his bed. "I do not deny knowing the lady, sir, I merely wished to correct an apparent misunderstanding concerning the degree of acquaintance existing between Miss Hinton and me. It is slight at best. I met her once when I was a youth, and then again a week ago."

"But what of Portugal?" Brad demanded.

"During that time, sir, I was unaware of her identity. And though I can never repay the debt I owe her, my only feelings for Miss Hinton are those of gratitude. Besides . . ."

"Besides, what?" Brad said, his hands balling into fists.

"Besides," the young man continued, the smile returning to his lips, "now I think of it, I am persuaded the lady loves another."

Unaware of the very interesting conversation that had taken place in the drawing room of Stoneleigh Park some three days earlier, Rosalind donned her walking boots, tied a gypsy hat of chip stray over her lace cap, and took herself for a solitary walk down the carriageway and into the lane. It was a balmy, late June day, and the sky was a clear blue. As well, the hedgerows were filled with tendrils of greenish-white bryony and fragrant pink and yellow honeysuckle, and yet, Rosalind saw none of it.

Too heart-sore to appreciate the beauties of nature, she walked purposefully, hoping to tire herself so she might sleep that night. She needed sleep, for since her return to Whitstock, every time she closed her eyes she saw Brad's face. She saw his blue eyes alight with devilment, heard his deep, wonderful voice teasing her, relived the joy of being close to him.

Hearing a carriage approaching, Rosalind snapped out of her melancholy long enough to search out a place in the hedges where she might step out of harm's way. To her surprise, the driver of the handsome dark green traveling chaise, reined in the horses just after they passed her. "Whoa," he called. "Whoa, boys."

The horses had not yet come to a complete stop when the door of the carriage was thrown open and a gentleman bounded out. He was a tall man, with broad shoulders and dark blond hair, and at the sight of him, Rosalind thought her heart would burst with joy.

It was Brad. But what was he doing here?

She had her answer within a matter of seconds, for he strode purposefully toward her, the expression on his handsome face resolute. Whatever his purpose, he did not intend to be gainsaid.

"Brad," she said when he stopped not three feet from her. "Why are you here?"

"For this," he said, drawing from the pocket of his corbeau coat a short, double-barreled pocket pistol. "Put your hands up," he ordered.

"What!"

"You heard me. I am a frustrated man, Rosalind Hinton, so you would be wise to do as I say."

"Frustrated?" she asked.

"Very. For a certain strong-willed, rash, incredibly beautiful female has been in my thoughts night and day, tormenting me so that I cannot sleep for thinking of her."

What could he mean? Rosalind's nerves felt stretched almost to the breaking point. Surely he did not mean that *she* was the one keeping him awake.

"And," Brad continued, "since that female informed me in no uncertain terms that she did not wish to be wed—that she would not have me—I am left with no recourse but to go back to where we began and start anew."

Rosalind began to tremble. He was talking about her. She had refused him. Not because she did not love him, but because he did not love her. And yet, he was here now, and the look in his blue eyes was making her shake like a blanc mange.

"I am still waiting," he said, raising the gun, pointing it in her general direction.

"Waiting?"

"For you to put your hands up."

Not certain what was happening, she did as he asked, raising her hands so they were just above her shoulders, the palms toward him.

"Very good," he said. "Now walk toward me. Slowly, until I say you may stop."

There was not that much distance to cover, but Rosalind took one step, then another, and another, until she was so close she could smell that clean, spicy aroma that was so much a part of him. She breathed deeply, filling her senses with his essence, and as she breathed him in, it seemed as though she could feel all the loneliness of the past weeks slowly dissipating. She felt a renewed joy taking hold of her soul. "What now?" she asked, the words suddenly breathless. "My hands are up and I walked as far as I can go."

He shook his head. "You can come another inch or so."

She obeyed without hesitation, drawing so close she fancied she could feel his energy, his strength pulling her nearer and nearer. "Now what?"

"Put your arms around my neck," he said.

Rosalind gazed into those remarkable eyes, and what she saw there caused her heart to leap. His entire focus was on her, and there was a question in his look—a question that set her pulses racing. "Like this?" she asked, placing her palms on his chest and easing them up and over his broad shoulders, then circling them round his firm, strong neck.

"Yes," he said, his voice noticeably husky, "just like that."

His arm slipped around her waist, gathering her just that little bit closer to him, and Rosalind thought life could offer no more joy than this, to be in the arms of the man she loved. When he bent his head and claimed her lips, she knew she had been mistaken—this was more than joy, this was bliss.

When Brad finally broke the kiss and looked once again into her face, he said, "I ask you again, Rosalind Hinton. Will you marry me?"

Warmth flooded every inch of Rosalind's body, yet still she hesitated. "I . . . I cannot marry a man who does not love me."

"Does not love you!" Brad muttered an oath then showed her the pistol again. "Madam, I came prepared to kidnap you if necessary." He tossed the weapon to the ground. "I am out of my head with love for you."

"You are?"

"Madly. Hopelessly. Foolishly. Why, I very nearly called poor Ashford out when I thought you loved him."

"You did?"

He did not answer, instead he untied her gypsy hat and tossed it to the ground then sent the lace cap after it. After staring at her hair for several seconds, he ran his hands through the locks, allowing the silken strands to curl around his fingers. "You are so beautiful."

"I am?"

"Very," he replied. "I thought that the first moment I saw you, when I woke and found you standing in my room, a vision in white. I believe I began to love you then as well, but I would not admit it, not even to myself, until we were in the village, and I saw you holding Senhora Duarte's baby."

He placed a series of soft, gentle kisses on her eyes, progressing slowly down her cheeks and finally finding her lips. "I saw you cradling that baby in your arms, and I knew instantly what I wanted: I wanted desperately to see you holding another child. Ours."

She slipped her arms from around his neck and wound them around his waist. Then she laid her head on his chest, hugging him as tightly as she could. He let her remain there for a time; then he put his hands on her shoulders and put her away a little, so that he could look at her. "I asked you to marry me," he said. "Will you finally give me an answer, or must I find that pistol again?"

"I will marry you, my love. No need to find the pistol," she said, "just find my lips again. Please."

ABOUT THE AUTHOR

Martha Kirkland lives with her family in Atlanta, Georgia. She is the author of four Zebra Regency romances: *The Gallant Gambler, Three for Brighton, The Noble Nephew,* and *The Seductive Spy.* Martha is currently working on her next Zebra Regency romance, *A Gentleman's Deception,* which will be published in June, 1999. Martha loves to hear from her readers and you may write to her c/o Zebra Books. Please include a self-addressed stamped envelope if you wish a response.

BOOK YOUR PLACE ON OUR WEBSITE
AND MAKE THE
READING CONNECTION!

We've created a customized website just for our very special readers, where you can get the inside scoop on everything that's going on with Zebra, Pinnacle and Kensington books.

When you come online, you'll have the exciting opportunity to:

- View covers of upcoming books
- Read sample chapters
- Learn about our future publishing schedule (listed by publication month *and author*)
- Find out when your favorite authors will be visiting a city near you
- Search for and order backlist books from our online catalog
- Check out author bios and background information
- Send e-mail to your favorite authors
- Meet the Kensington staff online
- Join us in weekly chats with authors, readers and other guests
- Get writing guidelines
- AND MUCH MORE!

Visit our website at
http://www.zebrabooks.com